OF WATER AND MOONLIGHT

Thunderbird Academy #1

VALIA LIND

OF WATER AND MOONLIGHT

THUNDERBIRD ACADEMY - BOOK ONE

Valia Lind

It takes courage to grow up and become who you really are.

— E. E. CUMMINGS

Have enough courage to trust love one more time and always one more time.

— MAYA ANGELOU

❧ I ❧

There are no guarantees in life, but I'm pretty sure this day has been the most embarrassing day of my existence. Not only have I snagged my t-shirt on the door, ripping a hole at the seam, I have also managed to knock not one but two students into the wall. It's like I've suddenly forgotten how to be a regular human being. Granted, being a witch, I'll never be normal, but all these stares are driving me insane. I am not one for being the center of attention.

It's the first day of school of my second year at Thunderbird Academy and I, Maddie Hawthorne, feel like I'm a new student all over again. Year one was nice. It was quiet. I kept to myself and hung out with my best friend. I read books over the weekends while I practiced magic in my room. Cool. Fun. Under the radar. Just how I like it.

But then, the Ancient evil started waking up right on the outskirts of my hometown, and our whole magical community has been put on high alert. Now, my best friend is not coming back. The school is in uproar because of the dangers right outside our walls. And, oh yeah, I've apparently become a celebrity because my sisters and I performed an older-than-dirt ritual that cast a hedge of protection around my hometown of Hawthorne. I didn't even

I

VALIA LIND

do that much, just allowed my water magic to be part of the elements of the spell. My sisters did most of the work. But that doesn't seem to matter. I was there, and therefore, I must've done some impressive magical things.

Now everyone knows about it, and it's like I have a target painted on my back. And front. And sides. They're expecting great things from me apparently.

That's what Headmaster Marković told me this morning while I was trying to hide the hole in my shirt.

"Maddie, we are very proud of you," Headmaster Marković said. "You did your coven a great honor by performing that ritual. There is great power in you, and I look forward to seeing where you go from here."

No pressure or anything.

"Watch it!" A shout snaps my mind back to present. I glance up in time to see a group of guys walk almost directly into a group of girls who are busy staring at something in front of them. There's giggling and hair flips, but I can't make out what has them so fascinated. The guys don't seem very happy to be inconvenienced and ignored. A few try to strike up a conversation when they see the girls, but it's a no go. I smile to myself, duck my head, and keep walking. I need to figure out my room situation. Typically, Kate and I would already have all this figured out, but her family has gone into hiding, pulling her out of school. This danger has set the whole world into panic.

When I get past the crowd of people, I see what all the fuss is about. Three guys are leaning against the wall in that nonchalant, cool way I've always found fascinating. I don't think I've ever been that cool even when I've tried. Which might be my very problem, but that's not the point here.

All three look to be around six feet, or taller. Dark haired and gorgeous, like a star-filled night. They could be on the cover of any magazine with their broad shoulders and messy hair. I can't see their faces, but I imagine them to be just as striking as their build.

I'm only a few feet away when one of them turns, his eyes

2

snagging onto mine, and it's like my whole world shifts. Light blue, like the sky after a rainstorm, they pierce right through me. I think this is the moment I've read about in books where the heroine is swept into an insta-love situation. But instead of a romantic encounter, like maybe a smile, I get a grimace and a hard glare.

My own notions solidify as the guy continues to watch me, and I meet his glare with my own. A flash of something else comes over his eyes, but it's gone before I figure out what it is, and then he's turning back to his friends.

That's fine. It's not like I'm a girl who attracts guys anyway. I've always been a little "too intimidating" as they like to put it. Even though I grew up with two older sisters, I've always been my daddy's girl. While my sisters focused on growing herbs and studying spells, I was more of a feral creature, running wild in the woods.

Since dad doesn't have any elemental powers, he taught me how to live off the land and how to take care of myself. Those times in the woods are some of my favorite memories from my childhood.

My heart grows heavier the more I think about him, and it's difficult not to let the tears fall down my cheeks. He's been missing for four months, and we have no idea what happened to him. Only that he was taken.

That's what this year is about. Finding my dad. I don't care about being popular or well liked. All I care about is learning everything I can about the Ancient evil that has risen and figuring out if they had anything to do with my father's disappearance.

The Ancients were kept a secret from all of us and only those who have in-depth knowledge of our history knew of their existence. That all changed when suddenly my hometown was assaulted by shadow creatures and then struck with incurable sickness. I went home over the summer to try and help. Which I did. But that one small spell is only the beginning. There is so much more to learn.

An announcement alert sounds, and the hallway grows silent instantly.

"Please report to the grand hall for announcements. This is not a request."

The voice sounds almost robotic, and it repeats another three times before it shuts off. There's a moment of stillness right before the student body begins to move. I follow the crowd, trying to keep my head down as much as possible. It's not working.

Thunderbird Academy. A place where anyone can be themselves. Yet, right now, I wish I was anywhere but here.

THEY WON'T STOP STARING. IT'S LIKE I HAVE A NEON SIGN OVER my head, and the moment I step into a room, it starts flashing. I keep to the back of the crowd, but it doesn't help. It's weird to be here by myself. I already miss Kate's spunky presence and her constant commentary on the Academy. I understand why her parents want to keep her close. A lot of students didn't return because of the dangers brought on by the Ancients.

I think back to the information I recently learned about the Ancients. They were the first to walk the earth. The creatures who created the magic within and around us today. But their selfishness and need for power drove them to evil ways, and they almost destroyed the world. Warring within themselves, they brought on apocalyptic events and nearly wiped this whole earth from existence. Such magic is draining, and eventually, they had to make a choice. They had to slumber to replenish their power, and we have been living without them for generations. Their story has become nothing more than a fairy tale told to little children to scare them into obedience. And then, the stories stopped completely. The only reason I even learned about them was because they were already awake.

A part of me wonders if they hadn't woken up, if I would even have any information about them. For some reason, their presence right under our feet was the biggest secret my parents kept from me. And even still, the only reason my mom knew about them is because of her position as the coven leader. No one else even had an inkling.

When they started waking up, the Elders thought it would only be near Hawthorne. They were wrong. That's not a mistake anyone will make again. *We* will never underestimate them again. Because whether my mom likes it or not, I am part of that solution now. It affects all of us, and that's not something we can hide from.

As I study the faces around me, I realize there are quite a few new ones. Just like with Kate, I know some didn't come back. Everyone is in the midst of this battle now. But there are a lot more people here than would consist of a freshman class. Faces I haven't seen before, both younger and older.

"Good morning, Thunderbird Academy." Headmaster Marković speaks up from the stage, his voice amplified by magic to be heard throughout the whole room. "Welcome back to another year. I know many of you have questions regarding the Ancients, among other things, and I will do my best to address all of them."

He walks across the stage, and it seems that his eyes meet each and every student before he speaks again.

"As you may have noticed, the school is over capacity. That is not a mistake. This school is one of the safest places in the world, and students have been sent here from other institutions for that exact reason." He pauses again, and I glance around. Everyone seems to be riveted. "Room assignments will be given out when you leave this room. You have each been assigned a roommate." There are a few murmurs at his words, but he's not deterred. "Yes, it will be a tight fit, but we will make do. Packets with your class information are already in your rooms. We will have mandatory weekly meetings to keep you updated. Please." He pauses, and I feel the heaviness of the moment fall across the whole room. "Follow the rules. Stay inside the grounds. We will keep you safe, but we will need your help to do so."

With those words, we're dismissed. The students begin trickling out of the room, but I stay pressed against the wall, mulling over Headmaster's words. For them to make a public announcement, it means the situation is much more dire than I thought. The one thing I know about grown-ups is they keep their mouth shut about dangers until the last possible moment. It's that whole trying-to-protect-us concept. Which I hate because I clearly can help, if only I was privy to a bit more information upfront.

I'll need to call my sisters and see if there are any developments. We performed the bonding spell over the town, but everyone knows it won't keep. Other towns have followed suit, and I'm sure the academy has their own sets of protective barriers. Headmaster wasn't kidding about that. This building and these grounds are hallowed, protected by generations of ancestors and their magic. But the one thing I've learned in the last few months is that assuming is the worst thing we can do. The Ancients are too powerful, and we're too unprepared.

I will not be unprepared again. That's a promise I make to myself right here and right now.

When I finally push from the wall and head toward the teachers handing out room assignments, I let that thought solidify within me. This school is a safe haven, but it's also a haven of knowledge. I may not be as strong as my sisters, or as experienced as my mother, but I will do my best to help. Whether they like it or not. After all, I have a few tricks up my sleeve, and I'm determined to use them.

2

When I open the door to my room, I have no idea what to expect. I've always thought I'd room with Kate, if the time ever came for that. Instead, a pretty blonde greets me with a tentative smile.

"Hi, I'm Jade," she says, standing in the middle of the room. We study each other in silence, assessing each other. She's about my height, with hair down to her collarbone. She has bright makeup on and a red cami and jeans. She looks colorful next to my dark t-shirt and dark jeans.

"Hi. I'm Maddie."

"Well, this is awkward," she says, after another pause.

"Glad you called it." I chuckle a little, shutting the door and walking to my side of the room. My name is on the packet lying on the bed. I rip it open and do a quick read through of the classes. I have independent study this year which means I'll have time to sneak over to the hidden library I found at the end of last year. That's a knowledge I have only been able to share with two people, both of whom are no longer here. Kate and Liam. While Kate is hidden who knows where, I know where Liam went. Back to Fae. That is one place more secure than the grounds of Thunderbird

Academy. I shake away the melancholy of missing my friends and look up as my new roommate speaks up again.

"Look, I don't expect us to be best friends or anything," Jade continues, "but I hope we won't be enemies."

I smile at that because I understand. I've heard horror stories about being roomed with someone who makes your skin crawl. I never thought I'd have to worry about it at Thunderbird Academy because we've always had our own rooms.

"Well, at least there's not three of us in here. Because that might cause some friction," I reply, and that earns me a smile. I'm not picking up anything that would set off any internal alarms in me, but I also don't dive in headfirst into trusting people. It'll take time, but at least we've broken the ice.

"Are you a transfer too?" she asks as she turns back to her side of the room and begins unpacking her suitcase. My duffle waits for me at the side of the bed as well. Part of the service provided by the academy.

"No, this is my second year here. Where did you come from?" As I ask the question, I realize that maybe she has no idea who I am. It's possible if she's not from around these parts. My last name is pretty known in the witchy circles, but there's a possibility I'm not as talked about as I thought. It's a nice reprieve.

"A small town in southern California called Idyllwild."

"I don't think I've heard of it," I reply, turning to lean against the bed. She moves around the room, placing a few items on her desk, including a framed photograph of what looks like her parents.

"It's not super known, but it's a good community. We've always lived there. It's in the San Jacinto Mountains surrounded by pine trees, which is, like, my favorite part. I went to a secular prep school out there and then took classes within the coven. But with the Ancients coming around, my parents wanted me somewhere safer."

She glances at the photograph then, a tiny frown forming

between her eyebrows that I can relate to all too well. I feel the same sadness anytime I think of my family.

"It's just the three of us," she continues, still looking at the picture. "I've never been away from home before."

"Don't worry, they'll be fine."

She looks up at me sharply, surprised by my nailing down her concern without even trying. I may not be a Reader witch, but I've picked up a few tricks from my sister's best friend, Krista. It's becoming easier to discern people's emotions the longer I do it.

"I'm worried about my family too. It's natural. It's not exactly safe out there."

And I don't think it's safe in here either. But I don't add that last part. I know Thunderbird Academy is more protected than most of the places around the world right now. Sure, there are other academies offering their campuses as protection. Magic schools have become sanctuaries. But a part of me is worried that by doing so, we've also become a bigger target.

"Well, maybe if you're not too busy later," Jade begins, shaking off the sadness like a pro, "you can show me around the academy?"

She looks hopeful and I get it. Last year, I was lucky to have Kate here with me. Jade doesn't have anyone. I think we can both use a friend right about now. So, I give her a warm smile before replying.

"Well, I'm claws sharp, and I have no problem with that."

Jade stares at me with confusion, and that's when I realize what I said. Shrugging a little, I explain.

"My dad and I have this running competition to see how many older phrases and slang we can discover and use in our everyday conversation. *Claws sharp* means having a lot of knowledge about various things."

Jade's laugh rings out, but it's not a mocking one. I can tell she finds it as amusing as I do.

"That's pretty great," she says, grinning. "You will have to translate though because I'm completely clueless in that area."

"Deal."

"Your dad and you must be close," she comments, as we turn back to our suitcases. My hands freeze, reaching for a shirt, a pang of hopelessness shattering my bravado.

"We are," is all I say, but she must hear something in my voice.

"Maddie?"

I can't exactly keep this a secret. I'm sure she'll hear all about me when we step outside these walls and into the rest of the academy. But for a second, it was nice to pretend everything in my life was fine. I turn to face her once more, resigned to the truth.

"My dad is missing. He's been missing for about four months now. We're not..." I stop, swallowing audibly. "We have no idea where he is or what happened. He was on a research trip for Ancient defenses and then he was gone."

"That must've been awful," she whispers, and her eyes flicker to her photograph before they're on me once more. She's clearly close to her family, so I don't have to explain how this hurts me.

"I'm going to find him though," I say, standing up straighter, determination fueling my words. "I will do whatever it takes to figure out what happened."

"I'll help anyway I can," she says, and I believe her. There's an air of kindness about her, and I decide to trust it.

Maybe having a roommate won't be such a bad thing after all.

⚜

WE FINISH UNPACKING, CHATTING ABOUT OUR LIVES AND covens, and while she's a lot more hyper than I am, I like her. I still haven't mentioned my last name. I know it'll come up eventually, but it's kind of nice having someone not know who or what I've done.

When a bell dings three times, I glance at the clock and see that it's dinner time. Jade offers me a confused look, and I motion her toward the door.

"Three dings means mealtime. They don't use the PA system very often, just to notify us of the beginning of the day, meals, and important announcements. If you hear continued rings, seek shelter. It means immediate danger."

"Good to know," she replies, nodding her head.

"Don't worry, they go over the rules in orientation. And I'll stick close to your side until you figure it all out. Plus, we have three classes together. That'll help."

"I have to say, I expected more magical classes," Jade comments as we leave the room and head toward the dining hall. A crowd of students is migrating that way as well, and it's really noticeable just how many more people are crammed within these walls.

"You'll have plenty of magical studies," I assure her, staying close as we make our way through the crowd. "Even regular classes like English and History always have magical applications. It's how the school works. Which I love, to be honest."

"I can understand that."

When I started here last year, I had the same thought. Why wouldn't I have potions or spell casting classes? But the headmaster, along with the teachers, want to make sure we have a proper knowledge of every subject in the world. After all, we live among the humans.

"It's a buffet style setup," I say, as we walk into the large rectangular room. There are floor to ceiling glass doors at one end which are typically open once the weather cools down a little more. Tables are set up throughout the space with the buffet at the opposite side of the room from the doors, near the entrance. It's a good setup, except when you have twice as many students present. It'll probably take a while to get food and find a seat.

I spy the headmaster standing next to Mr. Olsen, the history teacher. They're conversing, but their eyes continuously scan the room. I'm not sure if it makes me feel better or worse having them here.

"So, are we going to talk about the fact that everyone seems to be staring at you?" Jade asks, as we get to the back of the line. I groan aloud, receiving a few more looks thrown my way, and a part of me wants to glare in return.

"I probably should've mentioned..."

"That she's a Hawthorne."

The deeps voice comes from my left, and I turn in time to see the guy from earlier step up to the line. He reaches past a few people, grabbing an apple off the counter.

"Excuse you, there's a line," I say, annoyance dripping off every word.

"Yep, I see it," he replies, moving past us and grabbing a few more items off the counter. No one stops him, which makes me even madder.

"Hello! You are not the only person here," I say, taking a step toward him. He turns, his eyes flashing as he does a once over.

"Eyes on my face," I snap, and they instantly fly up to meet my own. A mask of indifference comes over his features before I can decipher any of his other emotions.

"Does Duchess have something to say?" he asks, and his voice burrows straight under my skin, irritating and exciting me at the same time. Why does he have to sound so good? That deep baritone is made for secrets.

"Don't call me that," I almost growl, taking a step closer to him. "In case you haven't noticed, there are people waiting. I don't know what kind of manner-less hole you crawled out of, but it's polite to let people in line be the first ones to get the food they've been waiting for."

"Wow, Duchess has some bite to her. Here I thought you were all bark." His friends step up then, and he hands over the food he grabbed before taking a step toward me.

"You're a jerk," I say, not backing down.

"Never said I wasn't."

We stare at each other for a second longer before he moves past me, making sure to keep a wide berth and then he is gone. I glare at his retreating back before I step back into line next to Jade.

"Wow, that was hot," she mumbles, keeping her voice as soft as possible. A school with all kinds of supernatural beings requires us to be a particular kind of careful. Shifters, for example, have amazing hearing.

"That was annoying," I reply, but she's still grinning at me. "What?"

"Nothing. I've just never heard of anyone standing up to shifters and live to tell about it."

"He's a shifter?" I ask, a little louder than I intended. Jade narrows her eyes at me for a second, contemplating.

"You have no idea who he is?"

"Only that when I first got here, he made sure to glare at me from across the room."

The line moves forward, and we finally reach the counter. Grabbing a plate, we begin piling on food. I'm so hungry, I'll have no problem finishing the salad and Mac and Cheese.

"Well, he was in the registration line with me, and I know his name is Aiden and he's a wolf shifter. And that he's hot. So are his friends. Is that a shifter thing?" The words tumble out of her, and I have to laugh.

"Maybe. The pack in our town consists of pretty good-looking men," I reply just as a table opens up, and we hurry to it. It's right by the glass doors, and the forest outside makes me think of Hawthorne and my family. The last time I walked through the woods, I was with them.

"I'm sorry I didn't tell you who I was," I feel inclined to say. I didn't mean to not tell her.

"I knew who you were, Maddie," Jade replies, shrugging, before she takes a bite of her sandwich.

"But you didn't say anything," I point out after a small pause.

"I didn't want you to feel awkward around me. What you guys did, it's pretty incredible. But it's a lot of pressure and responsibility to carry around with you. You clearly need a break from all the scrutiny."

I stare at her, completely in shock. It's kind of what Kate would say if she were here. A grin splits my lips.

"I think I love you," I say, and then we burst out laughing. It's much needed after the day I've had, and maybe it's not the most embarrassing day of my life after all. It was a pretty full one though. I managed to make a friend and an enemy. I wonder what comes next.

ॐ 3 ॐ

The first week of classes is pretty uneventful but busy. Every teacher has given us their course curriculum, freaking me out at how much work there is to be done. I've had no time for my own research. When Saturday morning comes around, that's all I want to do. Figuring out how to sneak over to the secret library, that's the real problem.

Jade is sitting at her desk, head bent over a history book. We have a few chapters to read, but she's actually pretty good at this, considering she went to a secular school. I know some other students are struggling because they've never been outside their coven or its teachings. But my roommate has adapted better than expected.

The whole secret library thing is a bit of a conundrum though. I have a feeling Headmaster Marković knows I've found something, but he hasn't really asked me about it. And the few times I tried telling him, or even my sisters, something always prevents me. I think there's a spell on the library, which would explain a lot. Except for why it was revealed to me. Liam and Kate have both been inside the room, and that is the only reason they know of its existence. Whatever the case with that place, I'm thankful I was the one to find it. If it wasn't for one of the books in that room, we never would've figured out that the ritual my sisters were trying to perform was missing an ingredient.

"I'm going to take a walk," I announce, getting off my bed. "I'll be back in a few."

Jade doesn't look up from her studies, just waves a goodbye in my direction. I really am starting to like this girl. It's not like I'm replacing Kate, who I still haven't spoken to since I've been here, but it feels nice having someone on my side. Especially since I have someone against me.

Actually, it feels like I have a lot of people against me. Jealously is a powerful emotion, and it seems like many students here have been displaying it towards me. Or resentment. Or something I can't even name. Aiden is on top of that list. Every time he's in the vicinity of me, I can feel his hot glare on my skin like a brand. Thankfully, we only have two classes together. So, I guess it could be worse.

Even now as I walk down the corridor, the few students who are out of their rooms give me a quick glance. I can't explain the reasoning behind it, but I won't be pushed into hibernating in my room. Even though it's one of my favorite activities. It will be my choice to hide away, and that's what I'm planning on when I reach the secret library.

The school has always fascinated me. It's housed in an old castle building, but it's far from ordinary. The layout, if looking overhead, is c-shaped. But every part of the building is unique. The central area near the front doors, which I'm passing at the moment, is of the old baroque style. It's very theatrical in its display with grand staircases on the outside and inside, on each side of the front door.

The rest of the castle can only be explained as eclectic. Dad and I actually did research on various styles used to make up the design of the building. The west wing, in which Jade and I room, is mirrored after the Neo-renaissance style. I had no idea that was a thing before I read up on it. Apparently, it was a mixture of gothic and French Renaissance. The east wing is more Neo-gothic, and there are spires everywhere. If I could describe exactly what all these styles mean I would say they are very extravagant. The creators of this place liked to be flashy, but I can't say I don't like it. It gives the school character and I love it.

The east wing is where I'm headed now, to the greenhouse built attached to it. Last year, I spent quite a lot of time among the different plants, researching potions and natural inspired spells to help my sisters. That's when I discovered an old cellar and the staircase that lead into the tunnels under the school. When I followed the pathways it took, I stumbled onto the greatest treasure. A library, much like the one we have back home, but filled with ancient texts.

The place looks like it could be inside the building with large windows and greenery on the other side of the glass. It's a circular room, filled to the brim with books. But when I tried finding a way to go outside, there isn't one. I'm not sure if it's glamour or what, but it's fascinating.

So lost am I in thought, that I don't even notice Aiden until I'm almost on top of him.

"Aren't you a little far from home?" he asks when we're only a few feet apart. I always have to prepare myself for the impact his eyes have on me. It's like he can look directly inside of me.

"Shouldn't you mind your own business, Aiden?" I don't think I've ever said his name before, and it jars me as much as it jars him. He stares at me for a second too long, and I feel it all the way down to my toes. Snapping myself out of our staring game, I move to walk around him when he steps in front of me.

"I *am* minding my own business, Duchess. You're in my hall-way." It takes a lot of self-restraint not to comment on the nickname again, but I don't. Because I know he enjoys the fact that it gets under my skin. Instead, I meet him tit for tat.

"I don't see your name on it," I reply, placing my hands on my hips. We're back to our staring contest, and if there is one thing my sisters and I have in common it's that we don't back down from confrontation. Mom calls it stubborn. Dad calls it hard-headed. I take both as a compliment.

"Maybe you should look a little closer." He takes another step toward me. There's now only about three feet separating us, and the effect of his closeness is more unnerving than that hated nickname.

"No, thank you," I reply, looking him straight in the eye, "I have more important things to do. Like count how many lime trees are in the garden."

If I wasn't watching him so closely, I would've missed the way his mouth twitches at the corner. I think I almost got to him and that elevates me. I take a step, but he's not done. He moves with me, continuously blocking my way.

"Is there something else you need?" I finally ask, giving him one of my sweetest smiles. He blinks at me a few times. I expect another fight, but just as suddenly as he appeared, he takes a step back. "Carry on, then."

I move past him without a second look and half walk/half run toward the greenhouse. I know for a fact this isn't his hallway. He's two stories up in the southeastern corner of the building. I overheard some of his pack mates talking about it in the dining hall two days ago. He lives to annoy me, and if I'm to survive his torment, I need to add a few more items to my arsenal.

But right now, I push all thoughts of him away and head to the greenhouse. The secret library awaits.

THERE ARE A FEW STUDENTS IN THE GREENHOUSE ALREADY working on their independent study projects. Since I'm a water witch, most of my independent study will be done by the pond on the east side of the property. A part of me is ridiculously excited, but another part of me is nervous. I'm only sixteen, and since my powers manifested when I was five, they've been unpredictable. What makes me nervous is the fact that since the ritual with my sisters, they've been pretty dormant. Still there, but it's as if they're taking a break.

Not that I would fault them, if that was a thing I could do. The ritual required the use of all five of the elements: Earth, Fire, Air, Water, and Spirit. The rest of the witches involved, my sisters included, had a powerful booster alongside them.

The soulmate bond.

As I walk around the different plants, waiting to sneak over to the cellar, my mind mulls over the legend. When I was younger, it was one of the bedtime stories my mother would read me.

Soulmates were a belief that there are two parts of a whole out there, and when one meets their other half, their hearts and magic are bonded to outrageous degrees. Up until seven months ago, this was just a myth. But then Connor returned to his pack and ran into my sister in the library. A witch and a shifter is not a union approved by many. Most of the time, it's looked down upon. But if I've ever met two individuals more perfect for each other, it would be them.

Then, of course, came Mark. A witch from another coven who swept my oldest sister off her feet. He and Bri are perfect for each other in every way, and it was their bond that awakened her active powers. I wouldn't say I'm jealous, I'm ridiculously happy for my sisters. But I am wishful. I can only ever dream about a connection such as theirs.

During the ritual, they had the soulmate bond on their sides. I didn't. Even weeks after, I can still feel the bit of drain on my magic, which I really hope will get replenished before I have to cast in public. I'm sure that'll go over well with the student body. A powerful witch with tiny magic.

With my mind going over everything, I don't notice the students moving out of the greenhouse until I'm alone. After another quick study, I walk over to the south corner of the room and move aside a few strategically placed palms. Then, I remove the wooden crate over the door, and I'm in.

The steps are pretty old, and the darkness is unnerving. But

I've come prepared. After arranging the plants and the crate so it's not noticeable right away, I descend into the tunnel. People aren't usually in this part of the greenhouse anyway, but I try to stay as cautious as possible.

I've only brought Kate and Liam down here, and both times it was out of necessity. When I couldn't outright tell them about what I found, I could only show them. A part of me was sad, considering I loved having the place to myself. But I guess that resolved itself out, considering here I am again, all alone, descending into the darkness.

After about a six-minute walk, I timed it at one point, I'm in front of the doors. They look like any doors back in the academy. When I place my palm against the wood, it shudders, before opening up.

When I step inside, it's exactly as I left it.

The ceilings are incredibly high, and the bookshelves line every wall. It's a circular room with a few desks and chairs in the middle. And piles and piles of books. The view outside the window is just as comforting as the smell of books inside. The forest is strikingly green and full, and it makes me wish I could go outside and explore.

Instead, I make my way toward the desk closest to the window. The last time I was here, I had about four books on the table, and I see that they're all still there. Sitting down, I leaf through the pages, as if acquainting myself with an old friend.

For the first time since I stepped back into Thunderbird Academy, I am truly alone.

The thought makes me breathe easier for a moment, before the onslaught of emotions assault me.

The pang of missing my dad hits fast and hard, and I almost double over. There hasn't been even a clue to his whereabouts since he's gone missing. All that was found was his suitcase in the hotel he was staying in, but no information on what he was doing there.

He should be home. He should be reading books and trying to

figure out how to fight the Ancients. But instead, he's gone, and for the first time in a week, I let myself feel it.

I miss my family. I miss my sisters. And I'm scared. All the time.

I can't let people see just how terrified I am, but I've experienced firsthand just how powerful the Ancients are. I can't pretend the fear away. But that's exactly what I've been doing. With everyone's eyes on me, I can't let myself breakdown. Even though I want to, basically at all hours of the day.

From the core of my being, I let it all go. So, when the tears start to fall, I don't wipe them. I let myself cry in this underground magical library as my heart misses my dad and breaks for the hole he's left in my life.

I cry for my family and the trials they continuously have to overcome to stay alive.

I cry for every person in this school and every family they represent.

Here, away from the prying eyes of the public, I let myself be a teenage girl and feel every emotion.

Because I know the moment I step back into the halls of the school, I have to put my brave face on.

4

"**D**o you think Mr. Olsen assumes he's the only one we have to do homework for?" I ask Jade as we head out of his class two days later.

"I feel like all the teachers assume they're the only ones giving us homework. But I can't deny I'm fascinated about this paper."

"You want to write about the infamous Salem witch trials?" I'm surprised. Most witches I know stay away from that subject, but Jade seems genuinely excited.

"I actually do!" she exclaims as we head to lunch. "It's such an interesting part of our history, and something that links us to the human world, even more so than they realize."

Of course she would be fascinated. She grew up in a mostly human community. And she's right about the connection. From what I know, most of those who lost their lives weren't even witches, but witches did their best to protect the humans from the stupid prejudice of the government. So many more lives would've been lost if the covens didn't step in. But I also know many still carry the heaviness of the knowledge that they couldn't save everyone. That's something I'm all too familiar with.

"Don't look now, but Aiden is staring again," Jade whispers as we grab our food and head to the table. I don't need her to tell me. I felt his gaze the moment we stepped into the room. It's like he's attuned to me, much like I am to him.

"I have no idea what his problem is," I say, before I raise my voice just a tad. "It seems like he needs a hobby. He must live a boring life."

I know for a fact that he heard me, even across several tables, because I swear, I can feel the air chill around me.

"You really shouldn't provoke him like that," Jade whispers with a smile. "But it's pretty entertaining to see you go at each other."

"Thanks," I reply dryly. "I'm glad someone is enjoying themselves at my expense."

Not that we've really "gone at each other". We've had three interactions total, and they went much like our first one. Or the current one. He glares, I poke fun, sometimes there's growling. But I'm not really mad at her. If anything, I'm mad at myself for letting him affect me the way he does. We've become these weird enemies, and I still have absolutely no idea what I've done to deserve it. One of these days, I will ask him. Until then, I will hold my ground.

I've only taken about two bites of my sandwich when the PA system sounds, and a robotic voice begins an announcement. But even before it can begin, it's cut off by the continuous alarm. There's a pause in the air while everyone tries to figure out what to do, and then everyone is on the move. Chairs are pushed back in panic as students begin to scramble for cover. Some begin to scream as bodies clash together, trying to climb over tables to get to the exits.

"Come on, this one means serious danger," I say, reaching for Jade's hand. Before I can take it, we're pulled apart by people trying to get out of the room. I have to shoulder my way through the throng, and then I'm grabbing her arm and tugging her behind me.

The moment we're in the hall, I realize we're never going to make it to our room on time. The larger number of students in the school makes it very difficult to move around, much less head to the opposite side of the building. I flatten us against the wall, trying to stay out of the way.

"We're never going to make it," Jade says, coming to the same conclusion. She looks at me with fear in her eyes, and I try to think. I need to find a place to hide. Somewhere we can protect ourselves. The rooms seal with magic once the residents are inside, and I can already see students pushing into rooms that are not their own.

"Come with me."

I twist around to find Aiden on the other side of Jade, his eyes hard. I open my mouth to protest, but he cuts me off.

"My room is closer. Come on."

He turns, heading toward the stairs, and now it's Jade who doesn't hesitate. She grips my arm and pulls me behind her as we weave through the bodies. With Aiden in front of us, it's much easier to make it up the stairs. Once on his floor, we race toward his room, stumbling inside just moments before the alarm shuts off. He closes the door, and the quiet slams into us. I can feel the magic of the school sealing us inside as we stare at each other, Jade and I breathing heavily.

"What's happening?" she asks, glancing between Aiden and me as the two of us continue staring at each other. He doesn't take his eyes off me when he answers.

"The school grounds have been breached."

JADE HAS BEEN PACING FOR TEN MINUTES NOW WHILE AIDEN leans against the door, and I stand by the window. I've been trying to see if anything is going on out there, but the lawn has been completely deserted.

"How can the school have been breached?" Jade asks for the third time, and I can't blame her. This is supposed to be impossible, but here we are. Not even two weeks into the school year, and we're already in lockdown.

"Jade—"

"There's—"

Aiden and I speak at the same time, and I glance at him in time to see him nod. I accept it for what it is and reach for Jade to bring her toward me, sitting down on the bed.

"The truth is, we don't know what's going on. Maybe this was a test. Maybe something set it off without it getting inside the school's grounds. There's no telling the possibilities. We just need to stay calm until we can know for sure." My soothing voice and solid explanations seem to get through to her and she nods slowly. Then, she stands, walking over to the window and proceeds to stare outside.

I can understand her concern. I'm worried myself. But I know better than to display that kind of emotion, especially in front of a shifter. I'm not about to let a predator treat me as prey just because I'm feeling weak. Folding my hands on my lap, I do my best to keep them from trembling.

"Not bad, Duchess," Aiden comments, still leaning against the door. He's been guarding it as if he's afraid someone is going to get in if he leaves his post. I throw a glare his way, but I don't engage. Instead I turn my eyes to the rest of the room, studying it fully for the first time.

It's not much to look at. There are no decorations, or personal items. Just textbooks and notebooks along with a cup full of pens. The beds are made, and the rest of the area is as spotless as if no one actually lives here. I have questions, but I don't want to ask those either. I just need to keep it together until the doors unlock, and I can get out of here.

"Really? No response?" Aiden isn't deterred by my silence. "I thought you were all about confrontation."

"What is that supposed to mean?" He knows he's got me, and I silently curse myself for giving in.

"Nothing particular. Just that you seem to like the spotlight. Being a hero and all."

I see Jade glance over at us, but she's staying out it. He watches me for a moment, waiting to see what I'll say. Instead of the anger I expect to feel, all I feel is tired.

"Look, my sisters are the heroes. They're the ones who are eager to be on the front lines of this. I'm more of a background noise," I reply, almost sighing.

"Right. Because sneaking out of Thunderbird Academy and bringing vital information to them in Hawthorne, before you participated in one of the biggest rituals known to man, is totally staying in the background." Aiden folds his arms in front of him, staring me down. Both Jade and I look at him as if he's lost his mind. For a second there, he doesn't sound like he hates me. There's a hint of admiration in his tone, and it punches me straight in the gut.

"What? They had a class on my life where you're from?" I ask, meeting his eye.

"I like to know what I'm up against." He offers it up like a challenge, and I feel his look across my skin. Even though I'm trying hard not to let him see just how affected I am, a tiny shiver races up my spine.

"I did what I had to do to help my family. That's all there is to it."

He watches me with a newfound curiosity, his head cocked to the side. I wonder what he sees when he looks at me, what it is he finds in me that he has to hate.

Before we can take this any further, a single alarm sounds before the robotic voice comes over the PA system.

"All students and faculty, please report to the grand hall. Headmaster Marković will make an announcement."

The voice repeats the command three more times, but Aiden and I continue to watch each other. I can't even begin to guess what he's thinking, but then, he pushes off the door, yanking it open. Jade hooks her arm through my elbow, and we follow him out in silence.

I don't know what's going on in this school, but I can add Aiden to the list of frustrating puzzles. He's driving me bonkers.

⚜ 5 ⚜

The grand hall fills up fast. Jade and I find ourselves in the back of the room, around the same area I huddled on the first day of school. For some reason, I expected Aiden to stay by us, but the moment we're inside, he moves toward his friends without a backward glance. I want to talk to Jade about him and the confusing emotions currently warring inside of me, but then Headmaster Marković steps up to the stage, and a hush falls over the room. He looks more tired than I've ever seen him, and it makes me more nervous than I'd like.

"I wanted to take a moment and put your fears to rest," he begins without preamble. "The school's grounds have not been breached. I repeat, they have not been breached."

A murmur goes through the room, and I have a list of my own questions rising to the tip of my tongue. Jade and I exchange a look, but we don't speak.

"The alarm was not faulty, and there was danger right outside our borders. We decided to initiate the lockdown for two reasons. One, to see how fast we can get the school under lock and key. Two, we needed the freedom to check on the threat without worrying for your safety. Know that your safety is always the priority here."

He pauses again, but no one even makes a sound. The whole room seems to be holding its breath, waiting for him to go on. He does that slow study of each individual before he speaks up again.

"I do not want to keep secrets from you. I want you to always be prepared and to understand that there are many dangers out there. Not all of them come from the Ancients. I would like to be able to tell you that nothing can touch us here, but that is not true. While this is the safest place for you, it is a place that has a target on its back. The Ancients know of these schools, and they will not rest until they penetrate each and every one of them. However, they are not our only concern. There are still those radicals who wish us harm. We have always stood on the border line of our magical world and the human one. It has always been up to us to keep the world safe. We just have to work that much harder at it now."

He takes a deep breath before he continues. A feeling of dread washes over me, as if I know something is coming. And his next words solidify that thought, chilling me to the bone.

"While this is not something you have considered for yourself, we are instituting mandatory combat training for everyone," the headmaster announces, and this time it's not a murmur that comes over the room. Everyone seems to be talking at once. The headmaster doesn't shush us, letting the students get their feelings out of the way.

"But most of us are not preparing for Task Force or protection detail after graduation," one of the witches closer to the front points out, her voice quieting the rest of the students.

"You are correct," Headmaster Marković says, looking down at her. "And while you do have your battle magic, sometimes an enemy cannot be defeated by it. Or by manmade weapons. I want each of you to be able to pick up a dagger or a sword and hold your own."

Jade and I exchange another look, but I don't even know what I can say. She looks scared, and I'm sure I do as well. Combat training is not something everyone is cut out for. There

29

is a reason only the select are involved in such intense training. There is a possibility our bodies won't even be able to handle the strain, although that depends on the intensity of the training. My mind catalogues all these facts as Headmaster Marković continues.

"You have all been paired with a trainer. The information will be in your rooms. Please report to your appointed place and time. While this is not something you chose for yourself, I do ask that you choose to excel at it. It may be the difference between life and death. Dismissed."

Jade turns to me, her eyes big and round. Most of the students have never used battle magic, and now, they're being trained for combat. There's a heaviness in the air as people begin trickling out of the room. No one seems to want to talk about it. As I study my fellow students, I see fear and apprehension mirrored in each one. So many thought this would be a safe place, and now, it's like we have nowhere to go. We're halfway to our room before my friend speaks up.

"They're making us into soldiers," Jade whispers, and I shake my head.

"We're already soldiers, Jade," I say, the reality of the situation clear in my mind. "They're just making sure we're competent ones."

⚜

"Do you have any idea who the trainers are?" Jade asks a few hours later, as we sit on my bed with the envelopes on our lap. There's no name on the paper, just a room number and a time. I am to report to the building on the eastern side of the property tomorrow at three o'clock in the afternoon. Which makes me a bit curious, considering most of the classes are in the main castle. From what I've heard, special permission needs to be given in order to work in the areas around campus. I wonder the reasoning behind this.

The other paper that was left on my bed is a note from my sisters.

We're fine. Everyone is safe. We miss you.

Just three sentences to keep me updated. I hate this communication lockdown more than I can say. When Headmaster announced it, I really thought I could handle it. But now, I just want to be able to pick up a phone and talk to my family. Right now is definitely not the time to be thinking about that. I tear my eyes away from the paper and get back to the issue at hand.

"I would guess the students training for Task Force," I reply, focusing on Jade. The Task Force is basically our magical law enforcement. Many go on to serve in human equivalent positions, such as police or FBI. Some stay as personal protective detail within different cities or towns. These are the best of the best, men and women who have spent most of their lives training for this. I can always spot them from across the room. It's an upper level program that requires extra classes on top of the regular ones everyone else attends. There's an exam after your second year, and if you don't pass it, you get moved to a different group. Until you can retest again. They're the only ones I can think of who would be up to this task.

"It's so weird," Jade comments, bringing my attention back on her. "I've never imagined myself using any of the defensive arts I've learned."

"Have you ever used battle magic?" I ask, genuinely curious. Most witches our age haven't. I've heard that some covens don't even teach it until later in life.

"Once. And it wasn't even a huge deal." I nod but don't prod further. Battle magic is a tricky subject. I know from firsthand experience, some witches don't like talking about it. I'm not about to push Jade if she doesn't want to talk about it.

"It's just so strange," Jade bursts out, turning to me. Okay, I guess she does want to talk about it. "I mean, battle magic is all instinct. Regular spells have words and rules, but with battle magic, it all comes down to feeling. It seems uncontrollable."

"You're right, it's uncontrollable and a little scary." She glances at me sharply as if she didn't expect me to agree. "But it's part of us, just like anything else. I think it's important we learn how to use it now and not when it's too late. We shouldn't be afraid of our magic."

"I've never met anyone like you," Jade comments, cocking her head to the side.

"What do you mean?"

"I guess it's probably because I don't know that many witches our age, but you seem to be wise beyond your years."

Playfully, I push her shoulder and she laughs. It's not as if I had a choice about growing up. Everything that has happened in the past year has taught me I need to take every lesson and learn from every situation. There is so much more to discover about my magic and the magical community overall. I want to be ready.

"One of the witches who now lives in my hometown," I say, getting back to the original subject. "Is a boxer. For fun. I've never met anyone like her. But she can take care of herself in hand to hand combat like no one I've ever seen. I think it'll be interesting to learn such skills here."

"You would." Jade chuckles, before getting off my bed.

"What is that supposed to me?" I narrow my eyes at her.

"Just that no matter how much of an introvert you say you are, you are always up for trying something new and exciting."

I smile at her, letting her words warm me from the inside out. It's something my dad would say, and I appreciate it that much more hearing it now. He's the one who taught me how to love the learning process and how to explore the world around me. I need the reminder, because most of the time, I feel as inadequate as they come.

"You know, Aiden was right," Jade says, keeping her voice soft.

"I don't think I ever want to hear those words again," I reply, but not unkindly. She chuckles, sliding a notebook off the shelf by her bed before turning to face me.

"You are a hero. It's in you. Which is why I know you will find your dad. You'll do whatever it takes. I just know it."

She sounds so sincere that I do the only thing I can do. I jump off the bed and give her a tight hug, letting her know without words just how important her friendship is to me. She clings to me just as tightly, and I think we both need this. Regardless of whether I said it or not, today scared me. And I know from the pit of my stomach that it'll only get worse before it gets better.

❧ 6 ❧

All morning and afternoon, the only thing I can think of is the training. Classes seem to drag as my mind is full of possibilities. A few students already had their first lesson and so far, there are no issues. As soon as classes are over, I don't even bother with lunch. I rush over to my room and change into a pair of leggings and a loose t-shirt before I pull on my tennis shoes and head toward the building.

Most of the school is housed inside the huge castle, but there are a few buildings scattered on the grounds, used for various purposes. I've never been in this one, even though it's the closest structure to the main campus. It's three stories high, windows on every side. It looks like it was once a barn that was later converted.

Once inside, I head to the third floor. The room I'm training in is the farthest away in the corner. When I step inside, I see two walls covered in windows. However, even though it's sunnier than anywhere else I've been today, it's a nice, cool temperature. With this many windows, it should be a sauna in here, so I'm thankful for whatever magic is keeping me from dying in the heat.

There is no one else in the room, so I do a few stretches before I head to the window and proceed to study my surroundings. This is a good vantage point, and I can see over the tops of some trees closest to the structure. From where I'm standing, I can see the pond and the tiny island in the middle of the water. A bit of my magic flares up as I think about running my hands through the tiny waves created by the wind, and it makes me smile.

When I hear the door open behind me, I don't turn around right away. But then, before I even do, I feel him there. Slowly, I raise my eyes as I look over my shoulder and I find Aiden standing right by the entrance. He doesn't look happy finding me here, and I wonder if he also wasn't told who he'd be working with. I wouldn't put it past Headmaster Marković to be secretive.

We continue our stare down, and I'm trying very hard not to be the first to break. I need every victory I can get when it comes to the shifter. I don't seem to get many. Aiden seems to come to some kind of a decision then because he finally leaves the doors and walks to the center of the room. After a moment, I come to stand in front of him, neither one of us ready to speak. He continues to study me, and it takes a lot of self-control not to fidget under his imploring gaze.

After what seems like an eternity, he rolls his shoulders and finally speaks. I count this as a victory.

"Have you ever had any self-defense training?"

His voice still gives me goosebumps, but now it seems to be followed by a shiver up my spine. I hate how he affects me, and I hate it more that my body has become a traitor when he's near.

"My dad taught me some basic moves," I reply, keeping my voice as professional as possible. The room is large, it can probably house a hundred people easy, but it feels like the walls are closing in on me.

"Such as?" he asks in that same spine-tingling tone.

"Knee in the groin, the heel of the palm to the nose, kick to the side of the knee."

Aiden nods as I rattle off the list, his eyes as unreadable as always. What I wouldn't do to take a peek inside that stonewalled facade. I would love to know what ticks him off, purely for selfish reasons. If I knew what got to him, I would proceed to do exactly that.

"We'll start with some basics and go from there," he says, rolling his shoulders once again. I don't think it's a nervous tick, but I've seen him do it a few times.

"Why do you do that?" I find myself asking before I can stop the words, and his eyes flash as he looks at me. But now that I've asked, I refuse to back down. Maybe even a few months ago, I would've said never mind or sorry. But I'm not that girl anymore. I can't afford to apologize for my curiosity. When I don't flinch away from his hard glare, he does the shoulder roll again, but surprisingly he answers.

"My body is looking for a shift." His answer is gruff and to the point, but now that's he's given me this small gift, I'm hungry for more.

"Does it mean the wolf is dominant?"

"The wolf is always dominant," Aiden replies, no longer looking me in the eyes.

"So, how do you suppress him?"

"It's not really suppression," he replies as he begins to circle around me. "I am one hundred percent me, and I am one hundred percent wolf. But when my—" He stops abruptly as if he's about to tell me more than he wanted. "It's complicated," he finally says, "and not why we're here."

Then, before I can figure out what his intentions are, he moves toward me.

"Defend yourself."

MY ARMS FLY UP TO HOVER IN FRONT OF MY CHEST, A WALL between him and me. When he's close enough, I thrust both hands out, pushing him back as I take him by surprise. It doesn't take long, and he's on me once more. My knee flies up, but he's prepared for me and deflects it. Then, before I can think too much about it, his arms are around me, and he's holding me pressed against him, my back to his chest. He lifts me straight off the ground, and I dangle in his arms as I try to find a way to get at him.

"Let me go!"

"I don't think that's how this works," he growls right into my ear, and I'm too frustrated to keep my body's response hidden. A shudder goes through me and he pauses. I take advantage of his hesitation and stop struggling, making my body go completely dead weight. The move surprises him enough that he stumbles forward, and before either of us can know what's happening, we're falling.

But Aiden is faster than gravity, apparently. He twists in midair, landing solidly on his back, with me still pinned to his front. A gush of air leaves him, ruffling the hair at the back of my neck, and then I'm scrambling off him.

When I'm about two feet away, I turn to see him still on the floor. Alarmed, I rush toward him, but recognize my mistake the moment his arm snakes out and grabs my foot. He pulls me down, catching me with his other arm, and then he shifts us so that I'm under him, arms pinned overhead, legs captured by his own body.

"Not fair," I whisper, his face just inches from mine. The blue of his eyes drinks me in, as if he's just as fascinated by the closeness as I am.

"Sorry, Duchess. But there's nothing fair about war."

I bristle instantly, squirming beneath him, which puts our bodies even closer, now with the added effect of friction. He growls and I freeze instantly. That was a purely animalistic sound, and I felt it everywhere.

"One of the biggest lessons you can learn is never to trust anyone. Your friend can become your enemy. Don't be afraid to hurt them."

There's something behind his words that goes straight to my heart. For the first time, I think there's genuine emotion in his eyes, and it makes me stumble over my own breath. We stare at each other, neither one of us ready to burst this tiny bubble we have found ourselves in. I don't know what possesses me to speak up, but I do.

"That's a very sad way to live." My words are only a whisper, but the moment is gone, and he's moving off me while he pulls me to a standing position in the same motion.

"It's a way of life that will keep you safe. More so than what your dad taught you about self-defense."

"Please don't talk to me about my father."

I'm not sure why his words hurt me, but they do. I rearrange my clothing, giving myself a moment to reign in my emotions. I'm not about to cry in front of Aiden. He's the last person I will ever allow to see my weakness.

"And why not? He clearly fuels your actions at the moment. Tell me why."

"I don't owe you anything."

"Maybe not. But I was assigned to train you, and I need to know what I'm working with."

"You already have a perfectly fine notion of me in your head. I would hate to ruin it with the truth." I finally meet his eyes, delivering the words with a glare. But Aiden isn't deterred. For a second, I think he might smile. But I have yet to see one of those on his lips.

"I know he's missing."

"You don't know anything."

"You think the Ancients took him."

"Of course they took him! Why are we even talking about this?" I turn away, ready to leave all this behind, but he moves in front of me, blocking the way.

"We're talking about this because until you learn to control your emotions, you won't be able to control yourself."

"Oh trust me, if I had no control over my emotions, you and I would have an entirely different relationship."

His eyes flash, and the intensity in them burns me to a crisp. I realize too late how that sounds, but I'm not about to take any of it back. He stands his ground, and I have no idea who's winning or losing anymore. I can't seem to figure anything out where Aiden is involved.

"Are you so sure it was the Ancients that took him?" His question surprises me.

"They've been messing with my family for months. It's what makes sense. Why are you so determined to keep me from thinking they're the bad guys?"

"That is not what I said."

"Then, what are you saying?"

"Look, everyone knows the Ancients aren't the only ones hungry for power. There's plenty to fear out there even without them breathing down our necks. Some are using this as an opportunity to further their agendas. We have to stay on alert and consider all options."

"So what?" I snap, throwing my hands up in the air. "You think someone besides the Ancients took my dad?"

"Maybe." Aiden shrugs, completely unfazed by my outburst. "All I'm saying is you can't just automatically blame it on them. That seems like the easy way out."

That sets my blood to boil. I get right into his face, our bodies just a few inches apart.

"Nothing about this is easy!" I hiss, trying to control my anger and magic, which is finally showing its presence. "My dad is missing, and I have no clue what to do about it. Maybe you don't know what it means to feel so helpless, but I do. I don't need a lecture on my emotions. I'm holding it together just fine."

Something flashes in Aiden's eyes, and it's as if, for a second, he doesn't hate me anymore. I think he almost reaches out, and I notice just how close we're standing and how heated my body has become. But then I'm the one who moves away.

"I think we're done for the day," I announce before Aiden can come up with another biting remark. "I'll see you later."

Surprisingly, when I leave, he doesn't stop me.

❄ 7 ❄

When Jade and I go to dinner, we opt to sit with a group of our classmates instead of at a table by ourselves. I know she noticed I returned much earlier than I should've from my training, but she didn't press the issue. I can tell she's bursting at the seams to ask. I'm sure I'll be getting the third degree later. But for now, I hide in the crowd.

"Is it true that the Ancients are as big as a house?" Noel asks, and I zero in on him. He's watching me carefully, but there's definite excitement at the prospect of an answer.

"Noel," Jade hisses, and he ducks his head. It's been kind of an unspoken rule that my friends don't bombard me with questions. I met Noel last year, but we were never more than casual friends to each other before. Now he's part of my friend group, and as I glance around at the rest of the people at the table, I realize they're all curious. Apparently, it took someone over two weeks to be brave enough to ask, and I resign myself to my fate. After all, if I can't talk to my friends, who else am I going to talk to?

"I haven't seen one that big," I sigh, before turning back to my food

"What about those ones that can shift but into anything?" Vera asks in her calm manner. Her wavy shoulder length hair swings as she ducks her head to take a bit of her sandwich, her light brown eyes focused on me. She's a second year like Noel and me, but she's a hawk shifter, so we didn't hang out last year either. But it explains her interest in shifters.

"It's possible."

"Have you see their minions? I heard they're like flying shadows." Christy pipes up, flipping her long black hair over her shoulder and leaning towards us. Christy is a transfer like Jade, but she comes from another academy school. It's smaller and only houses witches. They disbanded when the danger became too much for them to handle, but Christy is the only one who came here. The others went into hiding with their families, much like Kate's family did. Not that I can blame them. This isn't exactly the safe place we were promised it would be.

"I have." I take a bite of my lasagna, hoping the conversation is over. But no such luck. I answered one question, I've opened the gates.

"How was it to be there, in the midst of it all?" Noel asks, leaning close to me. He's sitting on my left while Jade is on my right, and I can feel her shooting daggers at him. I glance up to find his face very close to mine, completely enthralled. But before I can answer, a shadow falls over the two of us. Noel and I glance up to see Aiden standing by our table, a hard look in his eye.

"We need to talk," he snaps, as if I've offended him with my very existence. I give him an annoyed look before I turn back to my food.

"Can't. Busy."

"I see just how busy." I glance over at him and find his eyes on Noel. Not for the first time, I wish I was a Reader because I'd like to know what he's thinking. He half growls at my friend, and I've had enough. Pushing back my chair, I jump to my feet before grabbing his arm. There's a collective hush over the table at my manhandling a shifter, but I don't care. I'm too angry to care. I pull him behind me as I march out of the room and into the hall-way, which is mostly deserted due to the fact that we're in the middle of dinner.

"What is your problem?" I ask, dropping his arm as if it burned me. It's true what they say, shifters run a little hotter than most beings. I can still feel the imprint of his skin against my fingers, sending tingling sparks up my arm, but I can't dwell at that at the moment.

"I don't have a problem." He shrugs, and it takes a lot out of me not to punch him in the gut.

"Oh really? You just enjoy growling at my friends for fun?" I place my hands on my hips, which is now my favorite pose when I'm around Aiden. He brings all kinds of responses out of me, ones that I'm not very used to.

"I wasn't growling."

"You were too! What has Noel ever done to you?" He seems taken back by my words for a moment, considering most people steer clear of confronting shifters. But if my sisters' significant others have taught me anything, it's that sometimes pushing a shifter's buttons is the best thing I can do. Even though it's dangerous. Aiden recovers quickly and is once again his stoic self.

"We need to talk," he repeats himself, bypassing my question. I roll my eyes as I fold my arms in front of me.

"So, talk."

He narrows his eyes for a moment, studying me in that intense way of his. But I don't back down. I've already decided that's the only way I will survive dealing with him. I have to give as good as he does.

"You ran out of training early today."

"That's not news to me," I comment when he doesn't continue right away.

"You're not making this easy."

"Did you want me to hold your hand through it? Whatever it is."

His eyes narrow again, glancing down at my hands, and I swear the temperature goes up a few notches. My mouth has a tendency to say things that can have double meaning. At least when it comes to Aiden.

"I'm trying to say I didn't mean to make you feel as if what happened to your dad wasn't important. I just get frustrated sometimes by how easily everything is blamed on the Ancient evil, when there is plenty of regular evil out there."

His outburst takes me back a little, and I think it surprises him too. It's more than he wanted to share, that's for sure. He's apologizing, in his own weird way, and I can see this isn't easy for him.

"I get it," I say, meeting his eye as I shrug. "People can be very single-minded about all kinds of things. Magic is one of them."

We stand like that for a minute, each of us unsure of what to say or do next. We haven't reached a truce, far from it. But the fact that he would come and seek me out, it shows promise of... something. I just have no idea what.

"Practice tomorrow?" he asks, his voice softer than I've ever heard it before. It tugs at my defenses, and suddenly, I can't speak. So, all I do is nod. He looks at me for a moment longer, before he walks away. I stand frozen for a moment, waiting for my extremities to start working again.

The way he looked at me just then... I'll be thinking about that long and hard.

"ARE WE GOING TO TALK ABOUT IT?" JADE ASKS THE MOMENT WE get back to our room. Once I could walk again, I made my way back to the dining hall and finished my dinner. My friends decided against bombarding me with any more Ancients questions, so instead we talked about school. But I knew Jade wouldn't let it rest, which was proved correct when we walk into our room.

"I don't know what you're talking about." I shrug, heading for my closet. As I pull out my pajamas, I can feel her eyes on me. When I turn, she's standing in front of her bed, waiting me out.

"Ugh, fine. What, Jade?" I sigh dramatically.

She giggles a little before running over pulling me toward my bed. She sits, turned toward me with an expectant look in her eyes.

"Yes?"

"Oh my gosh, Maddie! You're the worst. Tell me what happened with Aiden. And what happened earlier when you came back like thirty minutes before you were supposed to be done with training. And you were all flushed. "

"I was not flushed," I argue, but maybe I'm protesting too much. Knowing what will come next, I try to speak softly. Not that it helps. "Aiden is my trainer." There's a pause, then Jade squeals and claps her hands. "Seriously, Jade. What is that reaction?"

"That reaction is you tumbling around on the mat, all hot and sweaty, with one of the hottest guys in school."

"Who hates me. Don't forget that part." But I can't help feeling slightly flushed right now at the mention of Aiden and me... tumbling on the mat.

"I don't know. There's a fine line between love and hate, no?" She wiggles her eyebrows, and I can't help but chuckle.

"You are a hopeless romantic," I say, which earns me another grin.

"And I'm proud of it. But seriously." She sits up a little straighter, a note of seriousness coming into her voice, "I've heard he's one of the best recruits they have. I'm not sure if he's doing Task Force after or what, but he's been trained from an early age. He's a great teacher to have."

"If only we didn't hate each other," I point out again, and it's her turn to roll her eyes.

"So, what was the dinner thing all about?"

I was kind of hoping she would bypass that, but no dice. I realize I'm about to add fuel to her theory with my reply, but I don't have a choice.

"We got into an argument at training. About my dad." She reaches over at my words and gives my hand a squeeze. "He came back to kind of apologize. To make sure I'll be in training tomorrow."

"Awe, that's so sweet."

"Jade." I give her my best glare, but she's not deterred. She's enjoying it way too much.

"He was very alpha in the way he nearly bit Noel's head off, did you see that?" I'm still not one hundred percent sure what that was about, but maybe shifters are just territorial in general. If I was to let my imagination run wild, I'd think it had something to do with me specifically. I'm sure that's what Jade is thinking, but I don't need any more help in that department. I think about him way too much already.

"Yes, I saw that. I made sure he knew I wasn't happy about it."

"Honestly, Maddie. I think you're the only witch I know who has no fear when it comes to shifters. The way you pulled him out of there? I nearly had a heart attack."

"I guess it's because of my family," I reply, shrugging a little. "I mean my sister is marrying a shifter, as soon as he asks her. Which I think may be soon. But they're adorable, and my sister's best friend Krista? She's marrying a shifter too. Although he's half Fae. And Mark's sister, the guy Bri is in love with, she's with a shifter too. So, I guess you can say they've changed my perspective on shifters."

"See? Romantic." Jade points her finger at me. "You're in perfect position to explore all this tension between Aiden and you."

"Get off my bed, weirdo." I laugh, and she jumps up to her feet. I don't want to think about Aiden in any way. When the heart gets involved, all reason goes out the window. I've seen that happen to my sisters, and even going back further, I've seen it with my parents. It's not like I don't want that kind of a relationship, to have someone in my corner twenty-four/seven. But I can't let myself get lost in the fantasy. Maybe I have a different outlook when it comes to shifters and witches, but this won't be that kind of a story. I have more important matters at hand.

For now, I pull out my history homework and dive into reading. After all, I'm at the academy to learn.

❧ 8 ❧

"You're not trying."

"I swear Aiden, if you tell me one more time that I'm not doing my best, I will blast you out of that window."

We've been at it for almost an hour, and I don't seem to be getting any better. I don't know if it's because of what Jade said earlier in the week or the way he looked at me, but I've been on edge even more than usual. We've had five lessons so far, and I'm still making no definite progress.

"Maybe that's your problem."

"Excuse me?" I round on him.

"When was the last time you released your magic?"

I freeze in my tracks, stopping whatever tirade I was about to unleash on him because I honestly cannot remember. My magic has been mostly dormant since the big spell a month ago, but I haven't even tried exercising it. I've been too afraid to see if I have any left.

"That's what I thought. It's been weeks since the ritual."

"So?"

"So, I think you need a release."

I'm pretty sure the images that assault me at that point have nothing to do with magic. Well... maybe just a different kind of magic. I really need to get my head screwed on straight. I'm becoming unhinged.

"We haven't had any spell casting classes yet," I say slowly, realizing that he may be right. I haven't channeled my magic since I've been back. Being around him, I'm more hyperaware of every heartbeat and every creak of the floor. Maybe it's my magic that's making me so unbalanced.

"Okay, show me what you got." He steps back, folding his arms in front of him as he watches me.

"Right now?"

"No time like the present."

I want to argue, I want to refuse. But I do neither of those. Walking over to my water bottle I unscrew the top before placing it back on the floor. It's been way too long since I've practiced my magic. I take my time as I head back to the middle of the room, concentrating on my breathing and keeping my mind clear.

I can feel Aiden's eyes tracking my every move, but I don't look at him now. If I do, I'm not sure I'll be able to keep going. This needs to be between me and my magic.

When I'm in the middle of the room, I take a deep breath and reach out. I feel the magic rush through my blood, energizing every part of my skin. It races to my fingertips and it's like welcoming back a friend. Instantly, I feel better knowing it's still there, one with my being. I open my eyes, calling upon the water, and it lifts out of the bottle and races toward me as if it's been waiting for the freedom to fly.

With a flick of the wrist, I leave it hovering in front of me. Another flick, and it begins to shape. It spreads out like a flower blooming. The petals dance around the center as I move my hand left to right and back again. After a moment, I bring my hands together, and the water is once again an orb, hovering in front of me. With palms touching, I twist my hands in a circle, creating a cyclone. Then, just as it's picking up momentum, I send it flying into the air above me, and it bursts like a firework, leaving behind hundreds of stars in the ceiling above our heads.

"That's incredible." Aiden's voice is only a whisper, but it reaches deep inside me and makes itself a home there. I turn toward him, thinking he's watching the water and my magical stars, but his eyes are entirely on me.

"Just a little magic," I reply, and suddenly, I can't take my eyes off him. It's as if I'm seeing him for the first time, and there's no one in this world but Aiden. My gaze roams over him, hungry to take in every detail. His dark complexion, his messy hair, his intensely blue eyes. The t-shirt that clings to his chest in all the right places. I watch as his arms flex, a muscle jumping in his upper arm, and then my eyes are on his hands. They seem strong and capable, as someone who can hold me and chase all the demons away.

My magic flares up, and the water around us explodes, tinnier than the raindrops, but they don't fall on us. We're surrounded in a sparkling bubble of water lights, and it's more mesmerizing than anything I've ever experienced before.

Aiden inhales and the movement of his chest spurs me into action. Tearing my gaze away, I raise my arm in the air and motion the water back into a sphere. Then, I walk over to the water bottle, and pick it up. The water rushes back in, and I seal it with the cap.

A heavy quiet falls over the room and I find that I can't turn around and face Aiden. My display of magic was unexpected, and I don't know what to do with the feelings he evokes in me when he looks at me that way. But it's not like I can hide from him in this large room with just the two of us in it. So, I force myself to turn around.

He's standing exactly where I left him, his eyes still on me. I can't begin to guess what's going through his mind. But we need to get back to even ground because I feel like it keeps shifting under our feet. I'd never call myself brave, but I take the first step toward him now.

"Shall we?" I ask, jarring the silence with my words. He seems to recover as he nods, stepping up to me. Without a sound, he attacks.

I know he's holding himself back, slowing down his moves so I can figure out what to do, but I'm still so new to this it's difficult to keep up. Aiden reaches for my hand and I twist into it, wrapping it around my torso, as I slam into his front with my back, my elbow at his gut. He catches the blow, pinning me against his body, and the heat radiating off him momentarily fogs my senses.

Aiden picks me straight up off the ground, and I remember to relax my weight. He's ready for me, but I slip just enough, and I throw my head back into his face. The move is startling enough that he drops me back to my feet, and I twist in time to deliver the heel of my palm to his nose. At the last moment, he snags my hand, pulling it behind my back, which puts my chest directly against his.

We're both breathing heavily, our faces inches apart. Something is happening to me, and I can't put a name to it. He was right of course, I'm much more focused after the magic release. But I'm also much more focused on him.

"That's better," he says, releasing me suddenly and taking a few steps back. "I think we're done for the day."

Then, without another glance my way, he's gone, and I'm left standing in the middle of the room wondering what just happened.

❈

THAT NIGHT, I CAN'T SLEEP. JADE WAS GONE MOST OF THE evening with a study group, which was a blessing and a curse. I didn't want to answer any more questions about Aiden, but I also didn't want to be left alone with all my thoughts. Which is where I am now, tossing and turning at two in the morning, trying to shut off my mind.

After a few more attempts, I give up. The rule is that no one

50

OF WATER AND MOONLIGHT

should be wandering the halls after dark, but I need to get to the library. Maybe putting myself into work will help.

Carefully, I slide out of bed and reach for my leggings and a hoodie. Both are black, like a lot of my clothing, and perfect for staying in the shadows. I don't put my shoes on until I'm out of the room and moving toward the greenhouse.

The toughest place to sneak through is right by the front doors. With the two staircases going up on each side, there's always a concern that someone is across the way. Since the Ancients started waking up, everyone has been on high alert, which means the school has extra patrols now. A lot of them are graduates who went into Task Force or protective agencies. Sometimes, the student who are in higher levels of training are assigned to participate.

I manage to get down from our floor and onto the main one without too many accidents. Luckily, I haven't ran into any shifters because they would be able to sniff me out, even if I am hiding. When I finally make it to the east wing, I have to wait a few patrols out, but then I sprint toward the greenhouse without a second glance.

Thankfully, no one ever patrols inside the greenhouse. I have to keep away from the floor to ceiling windows, since there are patrols outside. Other than that, I just need to make sure I don't make any noise moving the plants and the crate.

Before I make it too far into the greenhouse, I pause. With the moonlight bathing the plants in its glow, it looks magical in here. I've never noticed just how many of the plants thrive in this atmosphere. My oldest sister, Brianna, would know each of these by name. I just know there are flowers that bloom only at night.

When a small noise comes from behind me, I'm instantly on alert. My battle magic flares up, coming much easier now that I've exercised it a little, and I start moving carefully past the row of plants. When Aiden steps in front of me, I nearly have a heart attack.

"Chicks on a raft! Do you have to sneak up on me?"

"You're the one sneaking around," he replies, his eyes sparkling in the moonlight. It almost looks like he's going to smile, but no luck.

"I wanted to come see the night blooming flowers." I pull out the first excuse that comes to mind, a little proud of myself.

"Nice cover. Also, did you just say chicks on a raft?" This time there is definitely amusement in his tone, and I can't help it. I like it.

"It's similar to eggs on toast."

"Still not sure how that relates to your current situation."

I shrug, probably enjoying this a little too much. But his question does bring with it quite a few memories. A part of me wants to share all of it with him, but I have to remind myself that Aiden and I are not friends. This isn't show and tell.

"It's something my dad says when he's surprised," I reply, going for the truth but keeping the emotions out of it. I don't need to break down in front of Aiden. He watches me for a moment longer before he nods, as if coming to some sort of conclusion. Instead of replying, he begins to walk around the greenhouse, looking over the plants. I feel like we lost some of our footing again, but then he speaks up.

"So, are you going to tell me why you're really here?"

I bristle at that, his tone ruffling my feathers. There's that footing I've been missing.

"If you don't believe my explanation, that's on you."

"I just know you a little better than that," is all he says as he continues to move around. Now it's my turn to follow him, a little peeved at his words.

"I'm not sure you know me at all," I announce, stopping near one of the blooming plants. Instead of looking at him, I study the flowers. I have to admit, they are worth the price of admission.

"Don't kid yourself, Duchess. You're not that complex."

That... that makes me angrier than I thought he could. Spinning on my heels, I face him head on, not realizing how close he's standing. I have to look up into his face, cursing his tall physique.

"You know nothing about me. You should really get your head checked out. I think you're becoming delusional," I state, my hands once again on my hips. He doesn't seem affected by me at all, yet here I am, all tangled up in little knots.

"You're honestly telling me you would risk reprimand by sneaking out of your room after lights out to come look at some flowers?" he asks, his words washing over my skin. He's so close, I would only need to move forward a few inches, and I'll be pressed against him.

The moment the thought enters my mind, I shut it down. What is wrong with me? I'm like a lovesick puppy all of a sudden, and I have no idea where it came from. I can make up a hundred excuses here, or extravagant stories, but for some reason, I settle for the truth once more. Maybe a part of me does want him to know me a little.

"If you must know, I love flowers. Any and all. They bring me joy. So yes, I would risk reprimand to come see something as unique and beautiful as a flower blooming in darkness."

My honesty descends on us like a blanket. I expect him to contradict me, or make another biting remark, but he doesn't. He studies me for a long minute, in which I try to keep my breathing as even as possible. Finally, he speaks.

"I'll walk you back to your room."

❧ 9 ☙

"**W**hat is one of the most recognizable events in human history revolving around magic?" Mr. Olsen asks the next morning. I've gotten so little sleep, it's difficult to stay awake. Even though history is one of my favorite subjects, my mind is either drifting to mine and Aiden's walk back to the room last night or just plain zoning out completely. We didn't talk on the way back, and even though I didn't tell him the truth about why I was in the greenhouse, I offered him a bit of an insight about myself. That's not sitting too well with me right now. He keeps winning, and I don't like it.

He's in this class, of course, so there's no escaping the fact that I can feel his presence. Even though I refuse to look in his direction.

"Come on, I know it's not even eleven o'clock yet, but someone give me an answer."

"Salem witch trials," Vera answers from the front. Mr. Olsen claps three times, stopping in front of her desk.

"Thank you, Vera. The rest of you haven't even started on your papers, have you?" I vaguely remember Jade mentioning this, and when I glance at her, she shrugs. I really need to check over my course curriculum to make sure I'm not missing assignments. I'm usually so good at keeping ahead of the curve. I can't believe after three weeks, I'm falling behind.

"Your paper, for those of you who haven't began their research, is about the effects the Salem witch trials had on our community. Specifically, how it affected you personally." He looks each of us in the eye before continuing. "What is one misconception that is known about the trials?"

This one I know, so I raise my hand.

"Miss Hawthorne?"

"That any witches were killed."

"And why is that?"

I realize everyone is looking at me now. I'm not sure what possessed me to answer, since I've been trying to keep a low profile, but here we are. Even though I won't turn in his direction, I can feel Aiden's eyes on me.

"Because those who were put on trial were simply humans under the influence of a fungus."

"Do you know the name of the fungus?" I'm waiting for him to move on from me, but he continues to watch me, waiting for an answer.

"Ergot." Thank you, Bri for making sure I had that knowledge stored away. I remember my oldest sister going on and on about the way people, human and magical, have a tendency not to treat plants in the way they should be treated. After all, we are elemental witches and our connection to the earth is what makes us so strong. Bri has studied plants her whole life and runs an herbal shop now. I've heard her Salem witch trials story more than once, and now I'm super glad I paid attention

"Very good, Miss Hawthorne."

He moves away then, heading back toward the front of the classroom.

"As Miss Hawthorne pointed out, yes. No actual witches were killed during the Salem trials. Those accused of witchcraft were found yelling and screaming and convulsing, spreading mass panic across the villages. Many of your ancestors were there and tried to help the best they could. It is a known fact that they healed and saved countless individuals who could've been dragged to court but were never even suspected. Sadly, they couldn't get to everyone.

Because of this one event in history, people outside these walls have an idea of witchcraft that is warped. With the rising of the Ancients, we're on the brink of another historical event. Some major events have already happened." Mr. Olsen looks straight at me as he says it, and I want to crawl under the desk. "Some are still in front of us. It is important that we don't allow outsiders to write our narrative. This is why I want you to do this paper. I want to hear your history and your family's history relating to one of the most well-known historical events. I think we can all learn something from it."

He dismisses the class then, and instead of jumping up and rushing out of the room, I take my time. Jade doesn't even question it, but matches my pace, as the rest of the class files out in front of us. I feel Aiden move past me, but I don't raise my eyes, and I don't react. After the room is clear, I finally glance up at Jade.

"We really need to talk about this, girl," she says, and I nod. I'm not getting out of this one.

๑๕๏

WE GRAB A COUPLE OF APPLES AND COOKIES BEFORE WE LEAVE the dining hall behind. Neither one of us feels like being inside at the moment, and the weather is just cool enough that we don't need to go back to grab our jackets.

Heading east away from the school, we enter lime avenue. It's a literal road lined with lime trees. Once spring hits, it's one of my favorite places because it smells amazing. However, we don't linger here now, but move past the trees and toward the pond. Dropping our bags on the ground, we take a seat right next to the bank. Being this close to a large body of water makes me feel elated.

"Maddie, spill," Jade says, as she breaks off a piece of her chocolate chip cookie. I chuckle at her words.

"Wow, let's just dive right in then."

"There's no other way." Jade shrugs in response. "You've been avoiding me all week. And don't think I didn't notice you sneaking out last night."

"Well, that's definitely not true. The avoiding you part." I bite into my apple, chewing slowly to prolong the not talking, but Jade is smart. She continues to wait me out until I have no choice but to give in.

"Oh, fine," I mumble, turning to face her as I criss-cross my legs in front of me. "Here's the short version."

I give her a quick recap of my week of training, including the magic lesson and the run-in last night. When I'm done, Jade is wearing the biggest grin on her face.

"Please don't do that," I say, turning to stare out at the water. I didn't quite mention how he's been making me feel, but I think she knows.

"I can see why you've been so cagey lately," she says. "Doing magic with a boy, tsk tsk."

"That's dramatic," I roll my eyes, but I realize she's right. Aiden watched me perform something that is sacred to me. He saw my powers as a display in front of him. Usually, that's only done between two people who trust each other immensely. I don't think I've ever showed off like that with anyone outside my family.

"You know, he has to shift in front of you now. That's the only way you'll balance the scales." I glance at her sharply. I didn't even think of that. I'm way out of sorts when it comes to him. Apparently even more so than I thought.

"I don't even know why he hates me, Jade," I find myself saying, my eyes back on the water.

"Maybe he doesn't."

"He does. I can almost feel it coming off him like steam. Ever since I met him."

"Now who's being dramatic?" she replies, shaking her head. "You don't know if he does. You only think he does."

"Well, he hasn't exactly put out the welcome mat."

"Neither have you," she points out.

"Okay, whose side are you on?"

"I'm on the side of the truth!" Jade puffs out her chest, saying the words as if she's proclaiming them to the world. Very dramatic and very Jade. "But also, I'm always on your side," she continues, lowering her voice.

I believe her. I've only known her for a few weeks, but I already can't imagine the academy without her. I miss Kate terribly, but with her in hiding, there is a piece of my heart that yearns for a friend. And I have found one in Jade.

"Have you heard from your parents?" I ask, turning the conversation back to her. I know she's been worried since we've been on a pretty tight communication lockdown. I haven't spoken to my family once since I've been here. Headmaster has been relying messages.

"I got a 'we're okay and proud of you' two days ago but nothing else."

I reach over, squeezing her upper arm in comfort as the sadness coats her voice.

"They're safe. That's what's important."

If anyone can understand being close to their family, it's me. Truth be told, I think that's what bonded me to this girl right away. There's something special in a person who loves and appreciates their loved ones. It's the kind of bond that speaks to me on a very personal level.

"Thanks, Maddie," she says, taking a deep breath. "It's just hard not being there. What if something happens? What if I can help somehow, and I'm so far away?"

"Trust me, that's something I understand all too well," I reply, closing my eyes momentarily. The feeling of helplessness isn't so forgotten that it doesn't bother me. I was here while my family was fighting the Ancients. I nearly lost my sisters and mom in the process. And my dad is still missing. "But," I say, opening my eyes and looking over at her, "All you can do is trust that your family knows what they're doing and that they won't hesitate to ask for help if they need it. It's the hardest thing, trusting that they'll be okay. But it's what we have to do."

"You're right. I know you're right."

"But it's not easy. I get it."

We fall silent then, each of us lost in our own thoughts. That desire to do something, anything, is almost overwhelming. I've been back to school for about three weeks, and I'm still nowhere near figuring out what happened to my dad. Not that I expected answers right away, but I can't even get down to the library to research. My sisters have given me no updates besides the very generic check in. All I wanted from this year was a chance to prove myself, to find something to help my dad. But so far, I've become angsty about a boy, who may or may not hate me, while I'm falling behind in classes. I'm really winning over here.

"Do you think...," I begin, but my voice is drowned out by the sudden sirens. Jade and I exchange a quick look before we grab our stuff and run.

10

We race past the trees, the siren sounding as if it's in our heads instead of all around us. I stumble twice, scratching up my palm before I right myself. Jade glances over her shoulder to make sure I'm following, as I try to catch up.

"Head for the training building!" I shout, because the castle is too far. I can't believe this is the second time we're nowhere near our rooms when the alarm sounds. This one seems to be even louder and longer than before.

Jade hears me and turns toward the building that's much closer. The feeling of danger intensifies with each moment, and then she's inside. But just as I reach the doors, they slam, shutting her inside with me on the outside.

"No!" I hear her scream and bang on the door. "Maddie!"

I hear a few more voices inside and someone shouting something.

"Jade, I'll be fine!" I yell, even as panic fills my chest. "Stay away from the windows and doors."

There's no time to hesitate. I push away from the doors, trying to orient myself. It makes no sense to head toward the castle. Everything is sealed with magic. But the school has to have a way to protect those who didn't make it inside on time. There has to be a work around for this. Except, I can't think of any. I will definitely have a few words with the headmaster after this is over. They should have instructions for these types of situations. Okay, I'm hyperventilating a little bit, I need to keep my head on straight.

I need to hide.

If this is an actual attack, standing in the middle of the meadow, completely in the open, is the dumbest thing I could do. Quickly, I weigh my options. My eyes zero in on the forest that surrounds the school's grounds, and I don't hesitate. I run toward the trees, pumping my legs as fast as possible.

A noise comes from somewhere behind me, as if a plane descending from the sky. I don't slow down, and I don't turn. If there is something there, it'll be easier to lose it in the thick of the foliage.

When I break through the trees in the next moment, I still don't let up. The need to hide drives me forward as the trees and the bushes get denser. With my momentum, I grab for the branch of the tree in front of me, catching myself as I swing onto it. It doesn't work the first time, and my hand stings from where I scratched it earlier. Instead of crying out, I take a deep breath and try again. This time, I'm able to hook my legs around it. Pulling myself up, I continue climbing until I'm far enough that I can barely see the ground.

My heart rate slows downs just a tad, but my senses stay heightened. I can still hear the noise, but it's centered more over the school than the rest of the grounds. I lean my head back, breathing in fully for the first time since the alarm sounded. I wish there was some way for me to know if the danger is real or if they managed to keep the school on lockdown. I look toward the direction I came from, but I'm much farther than I thought because I can't even glimpse the school through the greenery.

With the exhaustion overwhelming my body, I get a bit more comfortable on the branch before I hook my arms and legs into adjacent branches for safety. I have no idea how far I am, or even what is in these woods. We are not permitted to venture out this far, which puts me at a disadvantage. The only thing I can do is wait it out. Even though I have no way to figure out if the danger has passed and if it's safe to return.

Time goes by slowly. But even so, I can't tell much because the trees are tall and thick enough to block most of the light anyway. My watch is in my bag, which I dropped somewhere on the way to the eastern structure. I have no way of knowing what's going on.

After a few more long moments, I decide I need to get back to the main campus. Being all the way out here may be safe, but it won't be once the sun goes down. The noise from the alarm has long since faded, and my limbs have become numb from holding onto the tree so tightly.

Taking my time, I half slide, half scoot down the tree, staying as quiet as possible. I'm sure there are predators in this area as well. At least that's what I've read. We're safe if we stay in the designated areas, but the woods have always been a place for special assignments. I've heard the fae come through the forest sometimes, and while I know Liam, most fae kind of terrify me. I don't need to attract any more attention to myself than I already have.

When I'm back on solid ground, I do a quick study of my surroundings. I'm completely turned around, but thankfully, my dad has made sure I will never be lost. Moss doesn't only grow on the north side of a tree, but it mostly does because of the lack of the sun. It likes shady spots, so as not to dry out. I run a hand over the tree trunk, finding the prickly green. The majority of it is on the opposite side which means north is that way.

I head in that direction, keeping my steps as light as possible. To be honest, I have no idea what I'm walking into when I get back to campus, and I won't lie to myself and pretend I'm not scared.

It's not even five minutes later that I realize two things. I am much farther than I thought I was. And I am not alone.

SLOWLY, I DO A THREE-SIXTY, SCANNING MY SURROUNDINGS FOR any type of danger, but I can't see anything through the trees. It's so dark in this part of the forest, it's as if the sun never shines, even though I know it's not late enough for it to set already. I'm being very dramatic, but I'm sure my nerves are making everything that much more intense. A part of me thinks I stepped right into the realm of the Ancients.

The heaviness hangs in the air, and every shift of the leaves and flutter of wings from a bird taking off, makes my skin crawl. Even back home, we don't venture into the woods. The Ancients are the original elementals, and their connection to the earth is much stronger than ours. A part of me wonders if they can connect to every aspect of it, like insects and animals, and will them to do their bidding. Now, I'm just freaking myself out. Pushing the thoughts to the back of my mind, I take another few steps forward.

That feeling of being watched doesn't go away, and the battle magic at my fingertips crackles a little as my heartbeat speeds up. I feel a presence and hear a ruffle of leaves as my body tenses, ready for action. All that time training is about to be put to the test. Even my magic is itching to be set free. But at the last moment, something stops me. It's as if a force reaches out to me, soothing my nerves and calming my spirit. I watch as the brush opens up and a gorgeous dark-haired wolf steps through the branches. My heart thuds in awareness, goosebumps traveling up my arms and over my whole body.

The animal is more beautiful than any I have seen before. His dark brown fur shines in the darkness, as if it carries its own glow. He's large, probably tall enough to come above my waist. He looks like he can rip me apart with just one leap. His eyes are trained directly on me, and that's when it hits me all at once.

"Aiden?" I breathe his name, half question, half awe, and it's like his body relaxes just a tad at hearing my voice. He steps

63

toward me and then we're only a few feet apart. We stare at each other, and I'm as mesmerized by his wolf as he was by my magic display.

Something changes in the atmosphere around us, an electric charge that races over my skin. It takes a fair amount of self-control not to reach out and run my fingers over his fur. I want to know if it feels as silky as it looks. Touching a shifter in his or her magical form is ridiculously frowned upon. There have been times where those who risked it were hurt in the process. But for some reason, I'm not afraid. A part of me knows that if I reach out, he would let me. It's like he wants to know what my hands feel like against his fur.

But I don't move, and he doesn't either. Because we both understand that's a line we cannot cross. Who knows how long we would've stood there if a howl somewhere deeper in the forest didn't break our concentration.

"I was heading back." I feel inclined to speak, thankful my voice comes out normal. He watches me for a moment longer before he turns and leads the way. I follow carefully, still keeping alert even though I sort of have a bodyguard now. Okay, not sort of. I am made in the shade with him by my side.

Another ten or fifteen minutes of walking, and the trees begin to thin out. I can almost make out the outline of the castle from here. When we reach the edge of the woods, Aiden stops.

"Aren't you coming?" I ask, looking over at where he positions himself. He shakes his head briefly, and a million questions rush into my mind. Something is going on.

But it's not like I can ask him anything, so I give him another searching look.

"Thank you," I manage, and once again, there's nothing but his intense stare. As I walk away, I feel his eyes tracking my every move. And when I finally do look back, he's still at the edge of the woods, watching me.

"Maddie!" Jade exclaims, rushing out of the eastern building and throwing her arms around me. My eyes are still on Aiden and when he sees Jade, he turns and heads back into the woods. "I was so worried. What happened to you? Once the lockdown was over you were nowhere to be found," Jade continues, pulling back and giving me a quick once over. "When the doors shut, I was so scared. I didn't know where you went. I started banging on the walls, hoping something would give. I even tried my magic."

"It's okay, Jade," I say, soothing her with my tone. "I know you did all you could." I definitely don't blame my friend for being left out of the building. That's on the headmaster and his lack of instructions for this exact scenario. My eyes roam over the people coming out of the structure while they head toward the main castle.

"Aiden didn't even hesitate to race out of there the moment the lockdown was lifted."

"What?" Her words stop me in my tracks, focusing my attention back on her.

"Aiden. He was in the building with me and he raced down and out of the building as soon as he could. Did he find you?"

"He did." I glance back over to the wood, but he's already gone. "I was already on my way back."

"Of course you were." Jade grins because I've told her about my father/daughter escapades. "But he still found you."

"I guess we're even now," I say, my eyes still on the trees.

"What do you mean?"

"I saw his wolf."

11

The school is in uproar when we finally make it inside the building. Two lockdowns in three weeks is a lot to take in. This is supposed to be the safest place for us, yet here we are.

"They haven't made any announcements yet," Jade says, as we push our way in the direction of our room. I can understand the panic these students are experiencing, even as I remain surprisingly calm. Being in those woods, all alone, was terrifying. But it was also a reminder that I am resourceful. I have to step up my game. No matter what, I am determined to make it to the underground library tonight. That place has helped me once, I truly believe it can help me again.

"Come on, let's wait in here." I pull Jade into our History classroom and out of the mob of students in the hall. By the time we make it all the way back to our room, we might have to come back anyway. She seems just as tired as I feel as she plops down into a chair.

"Education is exhausting," she comments, and I can't help but grin. It's such a random comment, and she delivers it so dramatically she should be in theater. We look at each other and then burst out in laughter, doubling over with amusement. Our emotions are so high, we can't seem to get control of them as tension seeps out with every giggle.

"The school is in danger, and you're laughing," The voice comes from the doorway and at this point, I'm not even surprised. I turn slowly, my eyes flashing.

"Three hundred and sixty-five rooms in this place and you end up in the same one as me. You know, stalking is illegal in all fifty states. And then some," I say, reaching for the comfortable hatred Aiden and I established on the first day of school because I desperately need to regain my footing. And not think about how much I want him to shift so I can see his wolf again.

"You didn't even look in here to see if it was already occupied. I could've been here first."

"No, you really couldn't have."

I know this because I would've felt him. I'm not sure when I became so attuned to his presence, but here we are. It's why I didn't attack in the forest, why I knew to trust a wolf I've never seen before. Something is stringing us together, and if I had an explanation for it, I would offer one up. But I've got nothing.

"What does that mean?" he asks, stepping farther into the room. His heated gaze is on me, and it's like he's branding me with his eyes. All air leaves my lungs, but I refuse to let him see just how affected I am.

"Wouldn't you like to know." I smile sweetly, and his eyes flash again, this time with so much emotion I nearly stagger where I stand. His gaze zeroes in on my lips, and I swear I can feel that look down to my very soul.

The moment becomes too much and not enough at the same time. If I could freeze time, I think this would be the memory I would want to hold onto the most. It's as if I'm seeing and feeling every emotion for the first time, and I don't know which way is up or which way is down.

I have no idea how our staring contest would've ended if the

PA system didn't crackle to life with its signature announcement ding.

"The student body, please report to the grand hall. Headmaster Marković has an announcement to make."

"We are spending way too much time in that room," Aiden comments, finally breaking eye contact. The moment he looks away, it's as if a weight has been lifted off my chest. I look over at Jade, who's still sitting in the chair, watching us like some reality show.

"Let's go," I tell her before I pull her up, and we head out the doors. I don't have to look back to know Aiden is keeping pace with us. When we all file into the grand hall, Headmaster doesn't wait for us to quiet down.

"Listen up," he begins, and I notice he looks even more rugged than last time. Normally, his suits are tailored to his very fit body. Even though he's got pepper in his hair, he looks strong and sure of himself, even at sixty years old. Now, he's wearing his age in a way that makes him look even older. Whatever is happening, it's more serious than I can guess. "I am sorry to say that someone is tampering with our protective wards. No one breached the boundary and no one will. But whoever is doing so is trying to instill panic into these walls and it's working."

"Is he saying what I think he's saying?" Jade murmurs beside me.

"There is a traitor amongst us." Aiden's voice comes over my shoulder, and those are my thoughts exactly. The headmaster promises they are doing everything they can to find out who the culprit is, but I'm not sure how this will play out.

Everyone within these walls is a suspect now.

"KEEP YOUR FEET PLANTED," AIDEN COMMANDS, CIRCLING around me. We've been at this for three days now, but I have no idea if I'm getting better. I've spent a few hours every night in the underground library since the last lockdown, still unable to find answers. There haven't been any more false alarms, but everyone is on high alert.

Aiden included.

He's running me harder than he has been, and I can't really decipher his mood today. He's angry at me for something, and I have no idea what.

"They are planted," I snap, as I bounce a little on the soles of my feet.

"Not planted enough."

He attacks, his arm aiming for my right side, but I shift quickly, bringing my elbow to block him. He goes for the left next, but I catch him there too. We continue the dance, moving left to right to left again, and I keep up with him at every turn.

"I'd say planted enough," I finally announce, grinning at him. He blinks a few times, as if he needs an extra minute to focus before he walks around me and toward where he left his water bottle.

"Really? Nothing? Not even a grunt of praise?"

"You want me to praise you?" He turns around quickly, getting right in my face. The outburst is so uncharacteristic of him, it stuns me for a second. But only a second, as frustration bubbles up inside of me.

"Yes. I'd like to be told I'm doing a good job when I clearly am," I snap, placing my hands on my hips and taking a step closer.

"I'm sure your attacker would be more than happy to mention your form while he's ripping your head off your shoulders." His words are dripping with sarcasm, but he's not the only one who has mastered that particular personality trait.

"Wow, don't have a cow. If it's such a bother to be nice for a second, you should invest in some etiquette lessons. Which I'm sure is too much for you to handle, so I'll show myself out." I grab for my own water bottle, taking a few sips before I turn toward the exit. We're done for the day anyway, and I'm not about to stand here accepting his foul mood.

"Don't have a cow? Who even talks like that?" He grumbles under his breath, but it's enough to have me spinning on my heels and marching right back up to him.

"I do. I talk like that. I also like phrases like peachy keen and tickety-boo. Do you have a problem with that?"

I'm right in his face, but I don't care. I don't appreciate being made fun of. And coming from Aiden, it feels ten times worse.

"No problem," he replies, raising his hands in front of him as if to ward off any more attacks. "You enjoy your random tickety whatever."

"I am enjoying it, and I would be very appreciative if you would stop making fun of me for it."

His eyes narrow at my words, and he drops his hands to his sides, suddenly deflated somehow.

"I'm not making fun of you."

"Really? So, what would you call it?" I stand as tall as I can make myself, not backing down. But I'm still not imposing enough, and I know it.

"I would never make fun of you for being who you are." He says it so softly, at first I don't think I heard him right. But the intensity of his gaze sends pleasant shivers up my arm, which I'm sure he notices with his shifter senses.

"Then what are you doing?" I ask after a small pause. He doesn't answer right away, as if struggling to find the right words. When he speaks, it changes something between us.

"I'm just trying to understand you."

We stare at each other, and it's as if all the oxygen has been vacuumed out of the room. A million questions race into my mind, the biggest of all is why? But I don't seem to be brave enough to utter that one word. My whole world has tilted with his truth and I don't think it'll ever be right again. The magic inside of me is just as restless as the heart beating in my chest. I know he can hear it, and I think his own matches my pace.

OF WATER AND MOONLIGHT

Then, just when I think I'm ready to move forward, Aiden rips his gaze from mine, taking two steps back. That's all I need to find my legs and head for the door, leaving him behind. Whatever just happened, I don't think either one of us was ready for it. But just like always, I leave feeling confused and unbalanced. But now, I add wishful to that list.

❧ 12 ❧

We're in the dining hall a few days later, sitting around the table, talking about our English project, when Headmaster Marković walks in. The whole room grows quiet immediately, all eyes on him.

"Good afternoon, students," he greets us, his voice carrying across the large room, clearly amplified by magic. "In light of recent events, morale has been incredibly low. To help combat some of the sadness that has descended upon this institution, I would like to announce that next Friday we are having a dance. Think of it as welcome back to school event."

Before he's even done, everyone starts talking at once. Headmaster Marković smiles at the room before he turns and leaves the way he came in. The energy has definitely gone up since before the announcement, it was fairly quiet in here.

"A dance! That sounds like so much fun," Jade exclaims from beside me. Christy is already nodding her head with more enthusiasm than should be able to live in that small body of hers.

Typically, I would be excited as well. It's not as if we have dances very often. Kate would definitely be the one jumping up and down if she was here. But lately, I've just been tired. I muster up a smile, but I don't really join in on the discussion as everyone begins making plans.

"Hey, I'm going to head back to the room and lay down for a minute," I say as I lean over to Jade when there's a small lull in the conversation. She gives my face a quick study and nods.

"Do you need me to come with you?"

"No, thanks." I smile. "I just need a little bit of rest."

I say goodbye to our friends and head toward the rooms, determined to sleep. Since I know I'll be sneaking over to the library tonight, I'm way too drained for anything right now. My classes are done for the day, and the training with Aiden isn't until four. I have a good four-and-a-half hour window that I am going to use to catch up on some rest.

But the moment I lay down on my bed, my mind begins working overtime. Shutting my eyes, I push all thought of my family, the Ancients, and especially Aiden, far from my mind, but it doesn't seem to be working. I toss and turn a few times, refusing to open my eyes. If nothing else, Mr. Sandman, if you're listening, bring me a dream.

Except, he doesn't seem to be listening.

I focus on keeping my breathing even, my eyes still shut, and my mind as blank as possible. But it doesn't seem to be helping. It's like my thoughts are being pulled toward one inevitable subject: Aiden. He's definitely winning the topic of obsession in my mind right now.

We've been in such a standstill for days now. Since his mini confession about trying to understand me, I've been even more unbalanced around him than usual.

I've never had anyone wanting to understand me before. At least no one who said the words out loud. There was something behind them too, some kind of an emotion I can't identify. But then, I can't identify anything when it comes to Aiden. He's so hot and cold around me, it drives me insane.

Forcing all thoughts of him out of my mind I move onto the next issue at hand. My father.

Bri sent a message yesterday letting me know Nolan and Krista are traveling to Nolan's home to see if the Fae have any information they'd be willing to share. Even though the message was delayed before it got to me, I can hear the underlying worry in her words. The Fae aren't exactly known for their hospitality, and Krista and Nolan are like family. At least Nolan is Fae, and pretty high up on the royalty ladder. That should offer him a little bit of protection now that he's back in their good graces.

I've learned that prejudice runs deep within magical communities. And not only with shifters and witches. Nolan, for example, is part fox shifter, part Fae. That earned him a banishment for a long while. The only reason I know all this is because his half-brother, Liam, and I became friends last year. Still, it doesn't sit right with me that Krista and Nolan are crossing into Fae lands. It's a huge risk to take, but I guess that's what happens when there is a war going on and your loved ones are in danger.

Now that I'm thinking about my hometown, my mind is once again with my family. I miss my father something fierce.

I would do anything to see his gigglemug right about now. The word brings a smile to my face as I think about the first time he told me about it. He was grinning so hard I thought his face would split in two. When he told me the word, I couldn't help but laugh.

"That right there is the exact definition of the word. A perpetual smiler."

There's no telling how much of it is true or how many definitions he's made up just to see me laugh. I squeeze the blankets close to my chest as the tears sting behind my eyelids. Something's got to give soon, and I'm scared it might be me. How many more sleepless nights can I manage? How many times can I sneak over to the library before I'm discovered? I'm not doing nearly enough to help find my dad, and the guilt is about eating me alive.

I'm not sure how, but with that thought, I finally drift off to sleep.

A CONSISTENT KNOCKING IS WHAT WAKES ME. AT FIRST, I THINK it's part of my dream. But then it fades before I can remember it, and the knocking continues.

"What?" I grumble, getting off the bed and yanking the door open. Aiden stands on the other side, his hand raised to knock again. "Are you lost?"

"Love the look," he comments giving me a quick up and down. I realize I'm wearing my Superman pajama bottoms and Batman t-shirt. "You know they're not friends."

"Neither are we. What are you doing here?"

That earns me a glare before he pushes past me and into the room. He heads straight for my bed, sitting down on it, arms crossed across his chest. I roll my eyes before I shut the door and turn to face him.

"By all means, make yourself at home."

"Thank you for your hospitality."

The fact that he can dish out as good as he gets is an admirable trait. And a very annoying one. I try not to fidget under his scrutiny. I'm sure my hair is a bird's nest. I never have learned how to sleep without waking up looking like I just fought off a sleuth of bears.

"You didn't show up to practice. I am merely doing my civic duty and making sure you're not dead."

I glance over at the clock, shocked to find it's almost seven in the evening.

"I guess I must've really needed the rest," I shrug, hoping he'll leave it at that. Of course, I should know better by now. He scoots farther up my bed, placing his back against the wall, his long legs stretched out in front of him.

"You really did. You looked like you were about to fall over this morning."

"Oh, Aiden. Haven't we talked about stalking and how bad it is for you? And most definitely me?"

I'm trying to keep calm about the fact that he's on my bed. His body is long and large, and it makes my bed look like it's child sized.

"It's only stalking if you don't like it, Duchess."

"Well, it's stalking when it's stalking. But if this is the reasoning you are employing, I am happy to announce that I don't like it."

If I wasn't watching him so closely, I might've missed the tiny spark of amusement in his eyes. It's so strange to me, but I have yet to see him smile. I wonder if he'll look like I've imagined him in my mind. Not that I'm fantasizing about him or anything. I'm just curious, that's all.

"You know, you wouldn't be so tired if you stayed in your room at night," he says, nonchalantly bypassing my comment and surprising me all at the same time.

"I have no idea what you're talking about," I reply, really wishing I could find a mirror and figure out what's happening on my head.

"Come on, Duchess. Do you really want to play this game with me?" He leans forward just a little, and my mind conjures up all kinds of games we could be playing. When have I become this person and when has Aiden taken permanent residence in my head?

"I don't want to play any games with you," I reply, keeping my voice steady. Reaching for my hair, I collect it into my hands before I start braiding it. He watches as my fingers make fast work of the strands, the look somehow intimate. He doesn't speak until I put an elastic at the end of it.

"You don't even believe your own words," he says, raising his eyes to mine once more. I bristle at that, because I'm not about to let him get away with telling me what I think or believe.

"Just because you don't want to accept defeat, doesn't mean I don't know my own mind," I snap, tired and frustrated and ready to have him out of my space. He's making my skin tingle, and I'm afraid I'll do something I can't come back from if he stays any longer. Like blast him with some battle magic. Or other things I don't want to put a name to.

"I would never dare to tell you what you think," Aiden says, scooting to the edge of my bed. "But I think you lie to yourself more often than you realize."

He stands then, and without waiting for a response, walks out of the room. I lean against Jade's desk, unsure of what exactly just happened. Anytime I'm around him, I lose all ground I've gained. He comes in like a hurricane, disturbing everything in his path, and I'm left holding the pieces.

When I walk back over to my bed, I realize I can still feel him on the sheets. There's a lingering smell in my personal space that's entirely his. I stare at the bed, torn between laying down and ripping the fabric off the mattress. Angry at myself for even thinking these thoughts, I grab my English homework and march to my desk.

I will study, and I will force myself to forget about the fact that Aiden was just lying on my bed.

❦ 13 ❦

The whole week is a blur of preparations. Everyone is asking everyone to the dance like it's homecoming or something. We typically only have three dances. The winter ball, the new year celebration, and the end of the year send off. Now, I feel like we're about to have a party every month, just to keep the morale up.

"You are never going to believe what happened," Jade announces, walking into the room late in the afternoon. It's Wednesday, which means we end the day in different classes, so I haven't seen her since lunch.

"Someone asked you to the dance?" I ask, barely looking up from my reading.

"How do you always know everything?"

"I wish I knew everything," I mumble, before placing a bookmark on the page and focusing completely on my friend. "Tell me *everything.*"

"Well, I was on my way to my last class and none other than Caleb steps into my path. But not in a weird way that made me run into him, just in a way that made me recognize he was in front of me. He then proceeded to ask me how I was doing and if I have a date and if I would be so kind as to go with him."

"And you said yes."

"And I said yes! How fun is that?"

"That's awesome, Jade. But I thought you'd be going with Noel."

"Umm," she turns away at my words, and I narrow my eyes.

"Jade. What are you not telling me?"

"Nothing."

"You are a terrible liar."

"Fine. Noel was going to ask you. Tonight, after dinner. You have to be surprised, and you have to say yes."

"Jade! Noel and I are just friends."

"Yes, which means you'll have fun together and can come with Caleb and me. It'll be great."

"Did you put him up to this?"

"I would never. He wanted to ask you, and I told him it's a great idea."

"Jade."

"Maddie. Come on. You cannot not go to the dance."

"I mean, I *could*." I was actually thinking about it because it would give me a good excuse to sneak over to the library. But now, I think I'll be scratching that plan off my to-do list.

"Madison Hawthorne, you wouldn't. It's our first dance together. We both have to go for that to be true." The pout she gives me is one powerful sort of magic because I can feel myself giving in. Plus, I know Noel and I would have fun. My mind drifts over to another boy in my life, but I scrap that before it can take root.

"Fine, fine, fine, I'll suck it up and dance the night away." I tumble back onto the bed, throwing a hand over my forehead.

"You are so dramatic," Jade laughs, and I know I just made her very happy. I guess it won't hurt to have a little fun once in a while. Just then, a knock sounds on the door before a letter is pushed under it. Since Jade is standing up, she grabs for it first.

"So, do we actually know how the whole note thing works?" my roommate asks, glancing down at the paper. "Is the knock attached to the magic that makes the paper appear under our door?"

"You're asking me this like I know the answer." I laugh, as she hands me the note.

"Well, this is your school." I shrug at that, glancing at my name written on the paper.

"It's a magical delivery system. That's all I've got," I reply, opening the envelope and pulling out the note. A huge part of me is hoping it's from my sisters, or Mama, telling me dad has been found, and I can breathe easier. But no dice. The note is short and to the point.

No training for the rest of the week.
See you next Monday. - Aiden

"What is it?" Jade snatches the note in alarm, reading it quickly. She glances up at me, a bit of confusion clouding her eyes.

"You looked like something was wrong," she says slowly, keeping her gaze on me. I try to shrug it off. "Maddie?"

"It's just weird is all. He's been so adamant about training. It's weird that he would cancel."

"Aha."

"Stop that." I point at Jade, taking the note back and dropping it on my desk.

"Whatever you say," she continues, before clapping her hands together. "But this is perfect because we can now pick out dresses together!"

"Dresses?"

"Yes! Since we can't leave campus to shop, they're bringing the shop to us. Today at four. I thought I would have to sneak a dress for you, but now I don't have to."

She's very excited and I can't exactly fault her for it. The faculty knew what they were doing when they announced the dance. Students have been in a state of elation for days. But as Jade settles down for her own studies before shopping and dinner, my mind drifts over to Aiden as my eyes find the note on the desk. It's odd for him to cancel. Something must be going on.

WHEN IT'S TWENTY MINUTES UNTIL FOUR, JADE BASICALLY drags me out the room and down the stairs. Her excitement is contagious, and I find myself getting into it. I've never been one for fluffy dresses or high heels, but that's because I spent most of my childhood in the woods with my dad. There have been a few times where I've dolled up, but all the major celebrations are reserved for after we've come of age. Since I'm away at school, I miss out on the summer Litha or the moon cleansing ritual. Thunderbird Academy has one of their own, but it's not until I've reached the upperclassman level.

"How exactly are we paying for these?" I ask, as Jade and I line up behind a group of girls. I see Christy and Vera closer to the front, and the shorter girl waves, while Vera throws a nod our way.

"We're not. They announced this in one of my classes. The faculty is supplying the dresses and dress shirts. They're even setting up a flower stand."

"How very teen movie-esque of them," I say, but not unkindly. It's nice to know that those who run this school are taking a personal interest in our lives. It would be so easy for them to just focus on the academics. But not only are they putting themselves in danger to protect us when the time comes, they're making sure we have a full high school experience.

"I think it's pretty amazing of them." Jade smiles, and I answer in kind. We move forward slowly, staying in line. It's a little surprising how organized this whole process is. I mean, they are dealing with a bunch of teenagers. But I love the fact that everyone seems to be on the same page. Maybe it's true what they say, and difficult times do bring people together.

When we reach the front of the line, we step through the doors to one of the classrooms which has been revamped to look like a clothing store. There are hanging rods set up all around with dresses, shirts, skirts, and even a few suits. On one side, they've also set up dressing rooms, with a few full-length mirrors. Currently, one of the mirrors is occupied by a pretty girl in a dark purple pantsuit. Her long blonde hair spills over her shoulders, and she looks powerful and ready for anything while the color complements her complexion.

"Wow," Jade breathes out next to me, and I glance to see her watching the girl. "She looks amazing. I could never pull that off."

"Me neither. I think she's one of the fourth-year students."

"Come on." Jade tugs on my arm, pulling me toward the racks filled with clothes. There are so many colors and material options, everything swims in front of my eyes for a moment. Jade begins pulling items out, happily holding them in front of her body for inspection. I take my time, walking down the aisles, hoping something will jump out at me. I'm almost at the end of the row when something does.

A tiny sliver of green material is sticking out between the reds, so I walk toward it, pulling it out more fully. The color reminds me of the forest around my hometown of Hawthorne, the fresh leaves mixed with evergreens. It's a floor length, off the shoulder, emerald satin beauty, and I'm instantly in love.

"You have to try it on." I'm so mesmerized, I don't hear Jade come up to me. I glance over my shoulder and she tugs my elbow toward the dressing rooms as I grab the dress. She's carrying three with her, purple, pink, and red. I have to say, I see her in the red.

I let her go first, and after she tries the others, red is the winner I thought it would be.

"What do you think?"

"I honestly love it," I reply, as she twirls in front of the mirror. From my sisters, I know it's a tea length strapless sweetheart cut. Harper wore one to her homecoming. The red reminds me of the apples we picked in the Autumn, and I squish the melancholy threatening to overwhelm me.

"I do too! Now you. I want to see that number on you." She

wiggles her eyebrows up and down, and I can't help but laugh. She brings the kind of lightheartedness to my life that I need right now. It would be too easy for me to get bogged down by my own mind.

When I step into the dressing room, I undress quickly. Once I pull the dress over my body, I know it's the one. It settles over my skin as if it was made for me. The length is perfect, touching the floor enough that when I rise to my tiptoes, it barely grazes the ground. The off the shoulder cut shows off more skin than I'm used to, but it also makes me feel as powerful as that girl looked in her suit. When I run my hands over the full skirt, I discover that the dress has pockets.

"Holy moly, Maddie," Jade says, when I step out to look at myself in the mirror. "You look incredible."

I do my own little twirl in front of the mirror, completely in love with the dress.

"Wait, does it have pockets?"

"It sure does!"

"Amazing!"

The fact that we're this excited about pockets just shows me I have no choice but to get this dress. It feels heavenly against my skin and makes me feel empowered somehow. I notice the line still out the door and quickly rush to the dressing room to change back. I think I could've stood in front of that mirror forever, and that's something new for me.

I've never been one to dress up because I never understood the importance behind it. I love what I wear, but it has always been more about comfort than fashion. That dress definitely showed me what a good outfit can do for my confidence.

"I can't believe we both found dresses," Jade says, linking her arm through mine as we carry our purchases toward our room. I'm about to answer when someone calls my name. I turn to see Noel heading toward us, and I know exactly what's about to happen.

"I'll just take that," Jade says, reaching for my dress before taking a step away.

"Don't leave me," I plead.

"Be nice," she replies, before rushing up the stairs. I turn in time to see Noel watching Jade retreat before he gives me a warm smile.

"Hey, Maddie."

"Noel. How's it going?"

"It's going. Do you think I could borrow your time for a minute?"

I want to say no, but I also don't want to hurt his feelings. I give him a nod and he leads me toward the front doors. Once we're outside, we head to one side of the staircase, away from the busybody onlookers. There always seems to be someone around.

"So, what's up?" I ask, ready to get this over with.

"I was wondering if you would like to go to the dance with me?"

His direct question takes me by surprise. I really thought he'd have to work up to it, but he just dives right in. I kind of appreciate it, to be honest. I already told Jade I'd say yes, but this makes me actually want to do so.

"I'd like that," I reply, and I can see him visibly relax. "But can I ask you a question?"

"Sure."

"I thought you'd ask Jade." That's not really a question, but I see his eyes cloud for a second, and I know I guessed it right.

"Maddie..."

"It's okay. I would still love to go with you, I just wanted to know if my suspicions were right. And I want to make sure you're going with the right person."

He laughs at that, which makes him look even cuter than usual. I can definitely see the appeal, even though I've never paid much attention before.

"Jade is going with Caleb."

"I know that." I watch him steadily, and he shifts from foot to foot.

"I was going to ask her, but he beat me to it."

"Why ask me?" I'm not upset, just genuinely curious.

"Because I consider you one of my closest friends, and I think we will have a blast together."

And just like that, my heart swells, and I realize how special he is to me. Somewhere when I wasn't looking, he's become one of my closest friends too. Without hesitation, I throw my arms around him, and he catches me easily. It's the kind of a hug that chases all the clouds away and fills the heart to the brim. I needed it more than I could've imagined.

❦ 14 ❦

The rest of the week flies by at the speed of light. The only noticeable drag is my lack of combat training. I'm trying not to let it affect me, but the fact that Aiden has gone MIA is keeping me a bit distracted. It also makes me search every hallway and classroom, waiting for him to show up. I'm annoyed with myself, to say the least.

"Earth to Maddie." Jade waves her hand in front of my face as Christy and Vera giggle in the background. The four of us are in our room, getting pampered for the dance tonight. The girls and I have all put on face masks, and Christy is currently painting Vera's nails dark blue. The shifter's dress looks like a galaxy and suits her perfectly. Christy chose a hot pink number, and I have to say, it's made for her. It's just as bubbly as she is.

"Sorry, sorry," I mumble, concentrating on the task at hand. Which at this moment involves picking out the perfect shade of lipstick for both Jade and myself.

"This one," I announce grabbing the tube out of the stack. "I don't think you can go wrong with a color called 'Firemen's Kiss'." Another round of giggles as Jade takes the lipstick and swipes it across her lips as a test run. Not to brag, but I can tell it's the perfect shade.

"You are a genius!"

I laugh, taking a little bow, as my heart squeezes in awareness at the scene in front of me. While I've never been much on makeup and spa days, my sisters, plus Krista, have done girl's night rituals much like these for years. They've always included me, even though I'm so much younger than them. Looking around, I feel that pang of homesickness that I usually keep at bay. I haven't heard from them all week, and on top of Aiden going missing, my emotions are at an all-time high.

"We should probably start getting ready with a bit more speed to our movements," Vera says, blowing air on her fingernails. "We're running out of time."

The rest of us glance over at the clock on the wall as Christy gasps.

"Vera! Why didn't you mention it sooner?" The other girl just shrugs, which is so like her. I don't think I've ever seen her lose her cool. Christy scrambles to her feet, rushing to the bathroom to wash up. There isn't much room to fit all four of us in, so we take turns.

Once my face is nice and scrubbed, I let Jade do my makeup. I could do it myself; I'm not a complete novice. Harper made sure her status as the second oldest sister was intact by teaching me all about eyeliner and mascara. But now that we're here, I want something more special. I could never achieve the perfect smokey eye, and I want to do the dress justice.

It doesn't take long for Jade to doll me up. She's a master, that much is clear by her every day striking looks. But when I finally turn and look at myself in the mirror, even I'm surprised by her skill.

My eyes look bigger, outlined perfectly in golds and silvers, making the green pop. The lashes are fuller than I've ever seen them, partnered with a subtle cat eye. There is a tiny amount of highlighter on my cheeks, just enough to make my skin glow. I realize we didn't decide on a lipstick when she moves in front of me once more.

"I think a subtle pink, almost nude color, will be best." She raises the tub at my eye-level, and I have to agree. The color reminds me of rose quartz, one of my favorite crystals. I'll be wearing a bracelet with the stone around my wrist.

"Now who's a genius?" I reply, letting her apply the lipstick as well.

The hair is next, and I do my best to curl it halfway down my back, before I pin it to one side. It's a look I've seen Bri do for one of her dances, and I've always wanted to try it with the right dress. When it's time to finally pull the material over my body, it almost seems surreal.

Each part of the process, from the cleansing mask to the smoothing of the skirt over my hips, made me feel empowered. I didn't do this for anyone but myself, and I tuck the feeling closely to my heart to carry with me forever. I just learned a valuable lesson, and I hope I never forget it.

When the knock sounds on the door, there's no hesitation as I pull it open.

Noel stands on the other side, black suit, white shirt, a green tie the color of my dress. I'm not sure how he found the exact shade, but he looks great in it.

"Wow, you look amazing," he says, grinning at me.

"You clean up pretty good yourself," I reply, answering in kind.

"Did they manage to talk you into heels?" Noel asks, a glimmer of amusement in his eyes. We had a whole lunch discussion about how I was not about to wear any sort of heels to this shindig. I would break my neck, and probably something else in the process.

"We compromised," I reply now, raising the bottom of my dress so he can see the black booties I have on. They have a small, two-inch heel on them, but they're wedges. If I needed to run, I'd be all good to go.

"Love it. It's totally you."

And with those words Noel chases away any reservations I may have had about the evening. He gets me, and I don't have to pretend or hide around him. That's what friendship is, being yourself with someone who understands you. I give him the biggest smile and he loops his arm to offer me his elbow. After a quick bye to the girls, I shut the door behind me. Without hesitation I place my arm through the opening and together we walk toward the ballroom.

※

I'M NOT GOING TO PRETEND AND SAY IT'S NOT WEIRD THAT MY school has a ballroom. Sometimes I feel like this place is right out of the late 18th century. I can almost envision Mr. Darcy and Elizabeth Bennett dancing right alongside us. The only thing missing is the candles as the only means of lighting.

When Noel and I reach the double doors, we line up behind all the other couples waiting to go in. I can hear music coming from inside and people talking and laughing.

"Is it me or is there a lot of pink?" Noel asks, as we study the people around us.

"It's not you." I reply, because girls and guys alike are sporting all kinds of pinkish shades. I've never been a huge fan of the color for myself, especially since it looks weird with my complexion. But some of them are really pulling it off.

"Oh, there's Jade," I say, just as my friend and her date finish descending the stairs. She looks incredible in the little red number, her hair swept up into an elaborate updo. The red lipstick is a perfect accessory to her dramatic cat eye. She looks like one of those Hollywood bombshells, minus the platinum hair, her shade is a little lighter. But it doesn't take away from her beauty I'm not the only one who thinks so.

"Wow." Noel's barely whispered admiration is not missed on me, and I give his arm a little squeeze. He tears his gaze away from my friend and gives me a sheepish smile.

"Don't worry, I agree," I tell him in a conspiratorial whisper. He visibly relaxes, but his eyes dart toward Jade once more. The boy really has it bad. But I honestly don't mind. Jade could do much worse.

"Come on," I say, pulling him toward the doors as the line moves. "You owe me a dance."

He grins down at me and then we're inside the ballroom. The place has been decorated with glowing lights all around. It's like standing inside of a gazebo on a Christmas night. It's magical and incredibly perfect for the atmosphere. I see quite a few Fae moving around the room, making sure everyone is having a good time. While we don't have many at the school, everyone knows they're good for throwing a party. Which is why all of them are on the party committee.

There are already people dancing. The music is a mixture of current and older songs, and I would be lying if I said I'm not getting swept up in all of it.

"Ah, there you are!" Jade comes up to us, pulling Caleb along the way. We're not friends, but he is in one of my classes. I've seen him hang out with Ben and Owen, two of Aiden's closest companions. Not that I've spoken to any of them before. Caleb greets us warmly, and I do have to say, he looks pretty good in his dark blue suit. What is it about shifters that they can wear anything and look like models?

Speaking of shifters, my eyes do a once over of the room, but I don't see him. It's foolish to even be looking for him. But I seem to have no control over that part. I could ask Caleb about him, even though I know they're not super close. But I resist. For now.

"Are we dancing or what?" I ask instead, and the group nods as one. We move toward the middle of the room, and it isn't long before Christy and Vera, with their dates, find us.

The base turns up and everyone around me cheers. Grinning, I begin to move, losing myself in the sound.

I have a secret. I love to dance. My sisters and I used to throw dance parties in Bri's shop, just to let loose. I remember it even as a six or seven-year-old. Harper would make the wind dance with us, making the chimes play us a sweet melody.

The energy is high, everyone jumping and dancing, and I feel like, for the first time, I'm just a teenage girl, enjoying her high school experience. There is no missing dad. No Ancient evil. No traitor within our midst. Just a bunch of friends, having a blast. My eyes jump from person to person, and I see firsthand the happiness radiating off them. I've found my tribe, and even though I still think of Kate, and even Liam, I'm thankful I have people around me I can trust and have fun with.

It seems like forever before the music slows and the lights dim, leaving only the twinkling stars all around us.

"May I?" Noel offers me his hand and I take it instantly. He pulls me toward him, settling one hand around my waist, the other still holding my hand. My body molds against him, and I rest my head on his shoulder, pulling him closer. He feels safe and stable. I could use more of that in my life right now.

After a few moments I raise my head to look at him and find him already looking at me. Maybe I'm getting swept away by the moment, but even so, I don't stop myself from speaking.

"I'm glad you asked me to come with you," I say, my eyes on his.

"I'm glad you said yes."

I look away then, because I'm not sure if I'm feeling something or not, but I don't want this to just be an in-the-moment reaction. Noel and I are friends, and I trust that over anything else. When my gaze lands on the crowd around us I find another pair of eyes on me. Aiden stands against the back wall, his eyes hard. He's wearing a dark button up shirt, with his sleeves rolled up and looks nonchalant and gorgeous at the same time. Then, Noel turns us and he's out of sight. When I look back, Aiden is gone. Maybe he wasn't there to begin with. I don't get the chance to find out because just then, the sirens start going off, and the rest of the lights go out.

❧ 15 ❧

There's a collective hush in the room, as if people are holding their breaths as one, waiting to see the legitimacy of the alarm. When the room shakes from some kind of an impact, everyone snaps into action. There are a few screams as some push others out of the way. The dark is making it difficult to see, and it's the shifters who have the upper hand. They begin shouting instructions while the older students move to the exits to direct people out of the room.

I can feel the fear in the room, especially from the younger students. A few of the teachers create an illumination orb to help dispel the darkness, but for some reason, it's not having as strong of an effect as it should. Something must be blocking the magic.

"Come on, we need to get out of here," Caleb calls out, and I feel Noel's hand wrap around my own. I glance over at him, but I can barely see him, even this close up. We call out to each other, linking hands, with Vera and Caleb leading the way. The doors seem to be a mile away, and the bodies continue to bump into us. Before we can reach the doors, another shock ripples through the ballroom, sending glasses flying, raining glass over all over us. A few cut my skin, and then another magical shockwave rushes through the room, bursting the ceiling fixtures and the rest of the glass in the room. My water magic flairs up on instinct, and I throw my hand in the air, pulling on the liquid and weaving it into a protective shield right as the shards reach us. Everyone screams, but the water protects the immediate group around me. I can't tell how far it extends, but I know it's not that large. Students are crying out, and even though I don't have shifter sense of smell, I know blood has been spilled.

"Neat trick," Jade comments as my friends huddle around me. I concentrate on the shield, and the shards that are caught in the liquid, before pushing it away. Without having light to guide me, I'm really hoping I'm not about to spill a bunch of glass and water on anyone. That's when I realize the outside doors are closer and to my right. Some of the moonlight can be seen through the blanket of darkness. I can push the water that way, but without being able to clearly see, I might make things worse.

"I need to get this out of here," I say before I drop Noel's hand and move with my magic.

"Maddie!" Jade and Noel both call out, but with just a few steps, they're lost to the darkness.

"I'll be fine," I call back, trying to reassure them. "I'll catch up with you in a minute."

It's taking most of my concentration to keep the shield high above everyone's heads. I can't see it, but I can feel how full of glass debris it is, and if I don't get it out now, I might be causing more problems. When I reach the outside doors, I open them with one hand, keeping the other outstretched above my head. The magic morphs and shifts as I walk through the opening, staying with me. A few shards of glass drop, but they're small enough that they don't cut me.

Once outside, I raise my other hand and then push the water and glass as far as I can before dropping it. I can't see much outside either, but it doesn't sound like anyone's out there. I'll have to remember to let the headmaster know what I did so some poor student doesn't end up walking all over it.

With that thought in mind I turn back toward the ballroom

and realize just how quiet it has gotten. Glancing around, I try to see through the dark, but the clouds must be obscuring the moon now, because any sliver of light there might've been has completely gone out. My eyes work to adjust as I look back and try to see into the ballroom, but there's just a wall of darkness. I take a few steps back, reaching for the handle, but it doesn't budge. I bang on the door a few times but hear no one.

"Great, just great," I mumble to myself, looking back out into the field and forest surrounding me. Without any landmarks to guide me, I already feel turned around. This darkness doesn't feel natural, and I wonder if this is another thing the Ancients can do. They can't penetrate the protective shield to come into the Academy themselves, but apparently whoever is on their payroll, so to speak, has been learning some new tricks.

Since the door is at my back, the front of the school must be on my left. Thankful that I opted out for my booties instead of the heels, I don't sink into the grass as I start to make my way there. As much as possible, I try to listen for any noises that might alert me to danger, but the silence is not disturbed. I leave my hand against the wall to help guide me, but that becomes problematic when I come to the bushes planted under the windows on one side of the building.

Taking a step away from the plants, I continue to walk straight, barely seeing few feet in front of me. I think I'm almost to where the building turns to the left, when I hear it. Something is out here with me.

I freeze in my tracks, my battle magic flaring up at my finger-tips. The rush of it sizzles under my skin, making me that much more aware of my surroundings. Even though I've been taught these skills, I never thought I'd be using them so soon. As Jade and I discussed, battle magic is all instinct. We don't have to say words to cast spells, it's literal electricity that runs through our veins. Some carry copious amounts with them and have learned how to unleash parts of their magic I can't even imagine. I can't deny how powerful my magic seems when I put a bit of emphasis behind it.

The noise comes again, but I still can't pinpoint it, or figure out exactly what I'm hearing. It's like a movement, just beyond my line of vision. A ruffle of cloth against skin? Maybe I'm feeling the eyes on me, more than I hear anything.

Then, when I think it's nothing but my imagination, a low growl sounds somewhere in the darkness, making my blood run cold. I'm not without defenses, but I can't fight something I can't see. I wouldn't stand a chance.

Slowly, and as quietly as I can, I move backwards. I'm trying to think strategically. With the building at my back, at least I won't have to try and keep that covered. Something glitters in the space in front of me, sending fear up my spine. I'm being stalked, there's no doubt about it and whatever it is, it can see me. Without a second of hesitation, I abandon my plan of trying to be inconspicuous. I bolt.

Whatever has been stalking me gives chase.

I GRAB FOR THE BOTTOM OF MY DRESS, PULLING IT UP SO I CAN run more freely. My legs pump as I sprint blindly into the darkness, one hand outstretched in front of me in case I run into something.

Glancing behind, I still can't see anything, but I can feel the danger. It's as if whatever is out there is playing a game of cat and mouse. I have a feeling I won't be as lucky as Jerry on this one. I've got no tricks up my sleeve, except for one. I can stop running and face this head on. But once again, I think of how much I am at a disadvantage. My dad would be disappointed if I didn't think this through first. He taught me to be smarter than this recklessness. I have to think. I have to.

I yelp as an arm reaches out to grab me, but instead of the attack I expect, I get pulled against a solid chest as the other hand lands over my mouth.

"Don't," a voice says as I struggle against the hold.

The whispered word is all I need to hear to know who it is. Aiden.

I stop struggling immediately as his arm tightens even more over my stomach before he removes the one covering my mouth. I'm tucked completely against him as he picks me up enough to spin us, tucking us into the space between the wall at the outer structure. Swiveling my head to the side, my cheek ends up pressed against his chest as I try to see into the darkness. But just like before, I see nothing. However, I feel safer than I've ever felt, in this moment, pressed against my sort of nemesis.

His breathing seems to match my own, his chest solid against my back. He's hotter than me, his body temperature raising mine. Or maybe it's his proximity. Even dancing pressed against Noel didn't feel this intimate. It's like Aiden and I are one, two beings in two different bodies, but breathing and feeling the same.

I think he feels it too, maybe realizes it at the same moment I do because he goes completely still. His hand on my stomach twitches, and I fight the sudden urge to place my own against it. Maybe it's the adrenaline, or the situation, but I want to hold onto him and never let go.

"Come on." His voice shatters our little cocoon of silence as he moves us out of our hiding spot. "We need to get inside."

But even as he says so, he doesn't move away from me. For some reason, I don't either. I turn my head slightly, glancing up at him, and find him staring down at me. My movement spurs him into action because he hastily takes a step away.

"We should...," he begins, his hand reaching toward me, but before he touches me, he stops. I'm not sure what's going through his mind, but I do the only thing I can think of. I close the rest of the distance and take his hand. There's a spark of electricity that races through me at the touch of his skin against mine, and I suppress a shudder. But just barely.

"Lead the way," I say, offering him a smile, which I know he can see with his shifter eyesight. He gives my hand a tiny squeeze before he starts moving.

We don't go too fast. He's taking his time to make sure nothing awaits us in the darkness. His grip on my arm is all the reassurance I need to keep my own heart rate down. I trust him to keep me safe, and that's saying a lot for someone who doesn't trust easily. Not where it truly matters.

After a few minutes, I realize we're not moving toward the academy but away from it.

"Aiden." I tug on his arm, ready to ask him the question.

"Not now," he replies before I can. Then, just as suddenly as he saved me the first time, he stops, making me run right into his back. My free hand lands on his waist, and it's his turn to inhale sharply.

"We need to move fast. Get ready."

I wish I could see what he sees, but even as I glance around, I'm completely useless out here.

"Now."

I don't hesitate. As he takes off, I keep up with him the best I can, trusting him to lead me blindly. When a structure materializes in front of us, I don't have breath left inside of me to ask questions. Aiden gets us inside before he shuts the door.

He drops my hand, and I can feel him moving around, as if he's making sure we're safe, before he comes to stand in front of me again.

"We're safe here for now."

"Where is here exactly?"

"One of the storage barns on the west side of the school."

"I didn't even know these were here."

"They're behind some of the trees planted along the walkway. Unless you come out here, you wouldn't know they're here."

Aiden heads toward one of the walls, leaving me in the middle of the room, unsure of what to do. The adrenaline is still pumping through my veins, but it's leaving quickly. I can already feel the onset of the panic I was repressing earlier. This whole ordeal, everything that has happened in the last few hours, it has left my emotions at an all-time high. I'm afraid I might burst into tears and not the pretty, delicate ones.

"Hey." Aiden moves so quietly that I don't notice him at my left shoulder until he's there, making me jump. "Sorry, come here." He takes my hands tentatively, leading me away from the middle of the room and toward the wall. Slowly, as if he's keeping his movements to a minimum, he sits down, tugging at my hand. Without hesitation I follow suit, leaning my back against the cool wood, Aiden at my side. Instantly, I feel better not being on my feet.

We sit in silence as I try to hear what's going on outside, but I have too many questions buzzing around in my mind. I start with the most pressing one.

"Are we really safe here?" I whisper, afraid to raise my voice any louder. But I know Aiden hears me, and I feel him move as he looks over at me.

"For the time being. Headmaster Marković placed additional charms around all the buildings on the property. Just in case."

"What's out there, Aiden?" I don't even bother masking the tremble in my voice. I don't think I've ever been more scared in my life. I always thought I'd be braver when the time came. But maybe I'm not as brave as I think.

"I don't know, Maddie," he replies, shifting again, and I can feel the brush of his shoulder against mine. The air around us is cooling rapidly, and my naked shoulders are covered with goosebumps.

"Are you cold?" Aiden asks because I'm sure I'm not radiating warmth right now.

"No."

"Maddie."

He really needs to stop saying my name because I can feel it at the pit of my stomach, like the butterflies all those books describe. I don't want to become a cliché, but he's making me feel things, and it's messing with my mind. I've come to know myself as

Duchess in his mind. The sound of my name on his lips breaks down all my defenses.

"Fine. A little cold," I finally say, before I feel him move once more.

"May I?" I turn towards his voice at the question and watch as he raises his arms, opening them up to me. I stare at him for a long moment before I scoot over and allow him to pull me close. The moment my back hits his chest I feel the warmth spread through me. His arms land around my shoulders, lacing over my stomach, and I'm cocooned in the safety of him.

For this one moment in time, we're not enemies or rivals. He holds me close, chasing away the fear and the worry. And for the time being, I let that be enough.

❧ 16 ❧

We sit in comfortable silence for a little while before the curiosity gets the best of me.

"What did you see out there?" I whisper, turning my head a little to look up at Aiden. He glances down at me, and I realize just how close our faces are. There's an intimacy to our embrace that makes my head spin, but I try to keep as still as possible.

"Nothing."

"What?" I jerk at that, sitting up a bit more fully so I can turn and look at him straight on.

"That's the thing, I didn't see what was chasing us. It was more like my shifter senses picked up on the being that was there, the danger it was broadcasting, but I couldn't find it. Even with my eyesight."

His words fill my mind with possibilities. My hometown of Hawthorne was attacked by shadow creatures sent from the Ancients, so I know they have a way of creating monsters no one has heard about. But this invisible attacker is something new. Something else occurs to me.

"But you know there's no one in here with us right now, right?"

"Yes, I still sense the creature the same way I would any danger, but I just can't *see* it."

I hear the frustration in his voice, and if I could see in the darkness, I'm sure it'd be written all over his face. He's allowing me this glimpse into his psyche, and I can't help but feel something toward his vulnerability. I don't think he'd ever give even this much of himself if the lights were on. Or maybe he would. Maybe he would for me.

"Where were you this week?" I find myself asking, and I can feel his body tense beside me. I almost wish I could take the words back because we were working toward something here, and I shattered it with my curiosity.

"I was on an assignment."

The tone of his voice shuts down any further questions, and I miss the small moment of camaraderie we shared. I want to lean back into his arms fully and find that peace again, but I'm too charged up now. And maybe, so is he.

"We should—" he begins, before he stops abruptly. I glance over at him and find his face in profile, staring at something I can't even imagine seeing.

"A—" I begin, but he places a finger to my lips, stopping the word in its tracks. Then, before I can figure out what's going on, he leans in, his mouth at my ear, sending a whole new batch of goosebumps up my arm.

"It's here."

My own body goes on high alert right before something slams into the structure. I yelp involuntarily, sliding back against Aiden as his arms come around me once more. He stands, lifting me in the process since I'm still pressed against him. He sets me on my feet but doesn't let go. Something slams against the opposite wall, but this time, I don't yell. I'm getting those sea legs back, as dad likes to say. I wanted to be brave, well it's about time I start acting like it.

"Can it get in?"

"I don't know, Maddie," he replies, right against my ear. "None of this is exactly playing by the rules."

I nod against him, placing my hand over where his is resting on my stomach. He tilts his hand, trapping mine under his when the building around us shudders. Twisting around, I try to pinpoint where the attack is coming from, but it seems to be coming from everywhere. When the hit comes again, the walls around us shudder, and I realize we are no longer safe.

"Aiden."

"I know."

"I don't know any protection spells," I mumble, feeling completely useless.

"It's okay. We need to move."

He reaches for my hand, giving it a firm squeeze as he glances down at me. I can't make out his look completely, but I can feel the determination rushing through his body and my own rises up to match his. Maybe this is the moment when we put all our bickering in the past and become something other than frenemies, but there's no time to get into it. I give him a firm nod before I let my battle magic unfurl within me. It seems to light me up from inside, the electricity zinging my fingertips. It might not be much, but this is one thing I can do.

"Ready," I say, and I swear he grins, right before he turns and sprints for the door. There's a slight pause, a moment of silence, and then he yanks it open. We race outside into the darkness, my dress tangling around my legs. I almost faceplant on the ground before he catches me, pulling me up. I reach for the dress, yanking the hem up, but that second of hesitation on our part cost us. Something slams right into Aiden, ripping him away from me.

"Aiden!" I scream, fear gripping me and making my blood run ice cold. My magic rises up as I search for moisture all around me. When I find it, I raise my hands, and with them the water, before I blast it in all directions. The moment it makes impact with something, I race toward the sound. There's a grunt as I get closer, and I realize Aiden is fighting something. I can't blast the attacker with any kind of battle magic without putting Aiden at risk, so I do the only thing I can. I throw my body completely at them. My shoulder slams into something solid, and I kick out the way Aiden taught me. The impact sends both their bodies in different directions, and I land hard, wind knocked out of me. The sense of danger doesn't go away but becomes heavier by the second. I sit up, trying to orient myself, but there's nothing but a sheet of black all around me. Aiden grunts again, and I twist around, zeroing on the sound before I blast my battle magic in the opposite direction, away from him. There's another yelp and then Aiden's arms are under my armpits, pulling me up.

Battle magic is tricky for someone with water magic. In theory, the stronger I get, the more likely I will be to summon whole rivers of water to protect myself with, along with the standard attacks. Right now, I do nothing more than push the attacker a few feet back. But it gives us enough time. Aiden is once again pulling me behind him, and I do my best to keep up. My body is exhausted from the running and the fear, but I can't give up now. The huge building towers over us in the next minute, the stairs just yards away. Aiden doesn't slow down.

When we finally race through the front doors, they open with surprising ease before we fall inside and shut them behind us. Just as the sound of the slamming fades, the lights flicker on.

I'M ON MY HANDS AND KNEES, BREATHING HEAVILY, WHEN Aiden's hand lands on my face, raising it to his.

"Are you okay?" he asks as his eyes roam over every inch of me. He looks like he's been through a battle. His clothes are torn up, exposing one of his shoulders, and his skin is marred by dirt. He's still the handsomest guy I've ever seen, and at first, I can't find the words. There's an intensity in his gaze that makes my eyes swim with unshed tears, and I don't even know what I'm trying not to cry about. But he sees the change in me, and so he does a very peculiar thing. He pulls me right into his arms, holding me close against his chest.

I don't hesitate to wrap my arms around his middle, burying myself in him. What we just went through, the almost certain death we almost came face to face with, I wouldn't have made it without Aiden. Without a second thought to how embarrassing I'm acting, I cling to him and he seems to hold onto me just as hard.

The noise of the academy coming to live around us is what finally pulls us apart. He seems to realize our position, letting go and getting to his feet in one swift motion. He reaches down to help me up, and when I place my hand in his, my whole body seems to sparkle. I drop it quickly, taking a step back as I try to smooth my dress out.

When I finally look up, his eyes are on me as he drinks me in. I have no idea what I look like, but I know my hair is a mess, and my dress is ripped in a few places. I wonder what he sees when he looks at me. There's heat in his gaze that warms me from the inside out. I'm almost afraid to breathe, if only to hold onto this moment for a little while longer.

A few shouts come from somewhere in the building before an announcement blares across the empty foyer.

"*The academy is once again secure. Please return to your rooms and wait for further instructions.*"

It repeats another two times, but Aiden hasn't taken his eyes off me. It's like we're in our own little bubble, and a huge part of me just wants to get right back into his arms again. Maybe I move toward him, or maybe he sees my thoughts written all over my face, but suddenly a shudder comes over him, and he's back to the cocky shifter I've come to know.

"We should really go over your self-defense moves," he says out of nowhere. "You've got some work to do."

For a moment, I'm speechless. But then that familiar anger at being treated like I'm on a different level than him returns, and I'm ready for battle.

"Is now really the time to get into this?" I ask, my hands on my hips. I'm not sure what I'm expecting, but I feel incredibly exposed standing in the middle of an empty room with only this flimsy green dress as the armor between us. I thought maybe we reached some new understanding, but it's like he's back to the detached instructor versus the caring... whatever he was outside of these walls.

"Sure, why not? Or are you so eager to get back to your date?" The way he says date is almost like he's spitting the word out. I'm having a difficult time following his train of thought.

"Do you have a problem with my date?" I ask, not backing down. That's something I'm never going to do when it comes to Aiden. I may be terrified of whatever monsters are hunting us, but I will not allow myself to be afraid of Aiden. If he wants to fight, then I will give as good as I get. I think I proved tonight that I'm not as fragile as I thought I was.

"No, if you like those kinds of guys."

"And what kind is that?"

"Soft."

"What you mean to say is nice and kind and who treat me with respect," I snap, not even bothering to hide my annoyance. Who is he to say what kind of guys I like? And who does he think he is to make Noel seem less than he is?

"I see you've got a real attachment to that one." He smirks, and I fight the urge to use some of those combat lessons on him.

"He's my friend, Aiden. Something you wouldn't know anything about."

I spin on my heels, ready to be done with this conversation. I need to make sure my friends are safe, and that I don't end up in trouble either. I've already wasted too much time.

"Whatever you say, Duchess."

"What is your problem?" I spin to face him, not realizing he followed me. I almost collide with his body but catch myself at the last moment. The memory of him pressed against me just a few moments ago is imprinted on me forever, and I try to keep my body from responding to his proximity. "Why do you treat me like I'm some plague of your existence? I'm not some doll to play around with. I deserve respect, not this strange hatred you seem to be carrying for me."

"Is that what you think I'm doing?" He seems genuinely taken back by my outburst. "I could never..."

I wait for him to continue, and it's as if he's struggling with something within himself. I see the battle in his eyes, and I almost reach out. But he doesn't speak, and it seems to bring him almost physical pain.

"Can't we be friends?" I whisper, my heart in my throat. His eyes flash with heat, before they're cold once more.

"We can never be friends," he says, his voice low and those five words hit me straight in my gut. I think I would double over if I was alone, but instead, I hold onto whatever is left of my pride.

"Well, now that we've settled that," I say, and this time when I turn to leave, he doesn't stop me.

❦ 17 ❧

Whe I reach my hallway, everyone is out of their rooms, completely ignoring the instructions. I hear my name being called before Jade pushes through the crowd, throwing her arms around me. She holds me tighter than ever, and I hug her back just as hard. My emotions are all over the place and while I didn't cry when I left Aiden, I still want to.

"Where did you go? We were so worried. I was terrified actually. What happened?" She pulls back, giving me a quick study as she gasps. "Seriously, what happened?"

Over her shoulder, I see the rest of our friend group move toward, and I give them a reassuring smile.

"I got stuck outside. Had to fight some invisible monster."

"By yourself?" Christy exclaims.

"Aiden was there." I shake my head, and I feel Jade's hand tighten on my arm. Before anyone can say anything else, the booming announcement sounds once again, this time ordering us to our rooms for the night.

"*The initial lockdown is initiated for the night. Return to your rooms now.*"

It makes sense they're taking extra precautions now, but it

doesn't make me feel any better. Everyone starts dispersing as Noel takes a step toward me.

"I'm so sorry. I never should've left you."

"You didn't," I remind him, giving his arm a quick squeeze. "I left to get the water and glass out of the room. That's on me."

He looks so contrite; I have the sudden urge to hug him. But something stops me. Maybe it's the memory of another boy holding me close just a little while ago.

"I'm okay, I promise."

He nods, and then he and Caleb leave for their side of the academy. Jade and I give the girls a quick goodbye wave, and then hand in hand, we hurry to our own room. The moment the door shuts behind us, Jade is pulling me toward the bathroom.

"Here, you can clean up while you tell me everything."

I glance at myself in the mirror, almost not recognizing the image staring back at me. My hair is matted and dirty, the bobby pins all but fallen out, just a few still holding on to dear life in my locks. My skin is marred by sweat and dirt, and my dress is completely ruined by the stains. One sleeve is barely there, ripped in half and falling halfway down my arm.

"Wow, I do look a little rough around the edges." I smile, but instead of playing along, Jade grabs my arm, squeezing it tightly.

"I was so scared, Maddie. We had no idea where you went and then they had to basically barricade us in some of the classrooms. There was this awful screeching noise that wouldn't let up for like ten minutes straight and some kind of thing kept banging into the building, making it shake. What is happening to this school?"

Tears are falling freely down Jade's face, and it's my turn to reach out to her, folding her into my arms. She may be one of the strongest people I've met, but tonight really got to her. And I can't fault her for that. Tonight really got to me too.

"It'll be okay, Jade. Somehow, someway it'll be okay. We have to believe that."

She clings to me for a little while longer, and I realize this is what my sisters would do. They'd hold me and tell me everything will be alright. Just then and there, I miss them so terribly it hurts. I miss my whole family, and I wish they were here to help me figure this out.

"Okay." Jade pulls back, wiping at her eyes. "Please tell me what happened."

And just like that, she's back to her curious self, and so I do what she asks. But first, I take a shower.

When I'm finally finished with my recap, we're sitting on our beds, in our pajamas, facing each other. My hair is still damp, so I braid it down my back.

"That must've been scary," Jade finally comments as I finish my braid and we both get under the covers. I reach for the light, turning it off, and the room is plunged into darkness.

"It was," I say, because it's easier to admit my weaknesses when she can't see me. "I thought I'd be better at conflict. But I guess all those rumors about me being a hero are exaggerated."

"Don't say that, Maddie," Jade replies, and even though I can't see her, I know she must be giving me one of her stern looks. "You came out on top tonight. You fought when it counted."

"Aiden helped," I admit grudgingly. "He more than helped."

"I think you give yourself less credit than you deserve."

"I just don't understand him, Jade," I huff, my thoughts once more on the strange way we left things, on how he did a complete one-eighty once we were inside these walls.

"He's a boy, I can't say I can help you on that one."

"He just gets under my skin so much," I say, my hands over my face. "I can't seem to find my footing when I'm around him."

Jade doesn't reply right away, and I wonder what she's thinking. When she finally does speak up, she takes me by surprise.

"Do you think maybe you have feelings for Aiden?" Jade asks, tentatively.

"Pfft. Yes. Feelings of annoyance and frustration and..."

"Maddie, I'm serious." I hear her sheets ruffle, and glance over in time to see her flicker on her bedside lamp. She's laying on her side, her eyes intently on mine. "You and him, you're more attuned to each other than anyone I've ever met. I know you have this rivalry going."

"Yes, he likes to push my buttons." I turn on my side, resigned to this conversation.

"He likes to push you. To be better. To be stronger. You'd have to be blind not to see it."

"Jade, you'd have to be a lot of things to think he cares about me at all." But even *I'm* not sure about that anymore. I remember the way he looked at me in my dress, the way his touch seared me right through. How he protected me without a second of hesitation. How he held me after we were safe. And how quickly all of that went away.

"He said we can never be friends, Jade. I think that sums up our relationship nicely."

I try not to show how much that still stings me, but it's difficult to push away the hurt. I thought we reached a new level in our partnership. I can't even call it a relationship, because that suggests a level of intimacy between two people. Yes, tonight we were on that level. But he shattered my every notion about us when he told me we could never be friends.

"Maybe he has his reasons," Jade draws my attention back to her. "We can't know what he's thinking. Or feeling. But I can tell you one thing, he's feeling something. And it's not hatred."

She lays back down then, turning the lamp back off, and I let her words settle over me as I stare up at the ceiling. I try not to let the hope blossom, but a big part of me wants to believe that Aiden and I are more than two people who were assigned to each other.

Jade might be right in her assessment of me. But I'm not quite ready to admit it to myself.

THE NEXT TWO DAYS ARE SPENT IN OUR ROOMS. WE ARE ONLY allowed out for meals before we're sent back to the rooms. It's a long and boring weekend, but at least Jade and I catch up on our homework.

When Monday morning comes, it's as if nothing happened. Everyone gets up, gets dressed, and goes to breakfast. There is an undertone of hushed whispers, but no one is saying anything outright. The whole school has been cleaned up as if the dance never happened. That includes all the broken glass. The dining room is in pristine condition as well, and for a second, I wonder if I made the whole thing up. Maybe it was just a crazy dream. But then I glance down at my left hand and find the few scratches I discovered yesterday, which brings up the memory of Aiden pressed against my body. I know I didn't make that up.

"Good morning!" Christy calls out as chipper as ever. Today she has on a bright pink polo shirt and a kilted skirt, completing her preppy schoolgirl persona. I've wondered before why Thunderbird Academy doesn't require uniforms, but I'm not about to ask and stir the pot. I like the fact that I can wear my dark t-shirts and jeans year-round.

"How are you doing?" Noel asks as I take a seat beside him. His eyes are intensely on mine, and I can see that he still feels guilty about Friday night.

"I'm peachy keen." I reply, giving him a bright smile. Well, as bright as I can muster. My attention roams over the room, and I realize I'm looking for Aiden. Forcing myself to focus on my friends, I catch Jade's knowing smile, and I shake my head at her.

"I know no one is talking about it, but can we talk about it," Christy mock whispers, leaning in. Vera nods her head beside her. Today the shifter has on a long, dark blue dress that has pockets in the front, with a scarf wrapped elegantly around her shoulders. She always looks so put together. I take a swig of my orange juice before I notice that they're all staring at me.

"I don't know what you want me to say."

"We heard you came face to face with one of them monsters," Christy comments, her voice sounding more southern than I've heard before. It's true that the accent comes out more fully when the person gets excited.

"I can't tell you much about that because I didn't actually see anything."

"Well I heard that—"

"Miss Ferguson." Mrs. Lee is suddenly beside our table, looking each of us in the face before turning her full attention to Christy. "The administration would like the students to keep from speculating. I would suggest you get back to your breakfast."

Then after another quick glance, the science teacher moves on. We don't say anything for a second, and I see that Mrs. Lee isn't the only faculty present. There are quite a few teachers roaming around the tables.

"Big Brother is watching," Vera says under her breath, in that dry humor of hers, and the rest of us giggle. It's not that this is a funny situation, but I think we're all wound a little too tightly.

"Makes sense why we haven't been hearing much talk," Noel says before he dives into his food.

I agree, the presence of the teachers is a little unnerving, and I'm sure people don't want to be whispering with them so close by. But I also know it won't last. We're teenagers after all. We have our ways.

When breakfast is over, Noel surprises me by falling into step beside us.

"Can I walk you to your class?"

He's never offered before. I know for a fact that his class is on the opposite side of campus. Jade and I have English this hour, while he has it third period.

"If you'd like," I reply, because I'm not sure what to say. It seems like he needs this. Jade gives me a puzzled look, but I just shrug my shoulders, and the three of us say goodbye to Vera and Christy before we head toward our class. We walk in silence, and I'm a little confused by Noel's behavior. Maybe what happened Friday night is getting to him more than I thought. When we reach the classroom, Jade slips right in, leaving me with Noel.

"Thanks for walking us," I say, giving him a small smile. He seems a little unsure of himself, as if he's trying to say something, but not sure how to bring it up. After a moment's hesitation, he returns my smile. But before he can say a word, Aiden is there, brushing up behind him.

"Sorry, mate," he says, giving Noel a tight nod. "But you are blocking the doorway."

Aiden barely glances at me as he says the words. Noel looks over and nods before taking my elbow and leading me away from the door. Aiden pauses at the threshold, but still doesn't turn toward me, even though it seems like he wants to, and I'm feeling uncertain once again. What is his problem?

"He seems in a mood today," Noel comments, bringing my attention to him.

"He's always in a mood," I say, not bothering to even lower my volume. I'm sure the shifter hears me. "Anyway, was there something you wanted to talk about?" I decide to face it head on.

"Yes." Noel seems to shake himself to refocus. "Could we talk after class?"

"Of course."

He gives me another quick smile and then he's gone. I walk into the classroom, heading toward Jade. As I do, I pass by Aiden's desk, and the boy has his legs completely sprawled out across the walkway.

"Do you mind?" I ask, annoyed, when he doesn't move his feet from my path. I glance over at his friends, Ben and Owen, but neither comment. I don't even know if I've ever heard Owen speak. Ben gives me a half smile but that's it.

"I sure don't," Aiden replies, shrugging. I roll my eyes and step over his legs, trying to keep my anger from showing. "You're making after school plans with your boy toy already? That was fast."

I glance over my shoulder and find Aiden's eyes on me. He seems completely at ease, but I've learned a little more about him in the past few weeks, and I can almost see the underlying tension in him. Narrowing my eyes, I surprise even myself when I take a step back and lean over, getting right in his face. My hand rests on the back of his chair, barely grazing his shirt as my hair, wavy from being in a braid, falls forward over my shoulder. His eyes track the movement, before they rest on mine.

"What I do is none of your business," I say, my voice low. His eyes flash, but I don't give him a moment to respond. Instead, I straighten, walking over to Jade and take my seat. The teacher walks in then, as I try to get my breathing under control again. A tap on the desk brings my eyes to Jade as she points to her notebook.

That was hot.

I grin at her hurried handwriting. I have to say, I'm a little proud of myself. When I face the front, I feel a few sets of eyes on me but none of them belong to Aiden. Owen however gives me a long look, and I think he's a bit proud of me too. I guess I like to push Aiden's buttons. I just may be getting better at it.

❧ 18 ❧

The rest of the day passes uneventfully. I keep expecting something to happen, but nothing does. It's like Friday night was just a normal part of the academy experience. But it doesn't mean I haven't been on alert the whole time. I think everyone is a little jumpy, especially since this is the first time we've been allowed to congregate again after the ordeal. When classes have finally ended for the day, Jade and I head toward our room, ready for a break. At least I am. The stares I weathered when I first came to school have returned. It's most frustrating.

"Maddie!" Jade and I stop as I hear my name called, and that's when I see Noel walking toward us.

"You know," Jade comments. "You probably should not be meeting in a public place. We wouldn't want Aiden accidentally mauling him." I glance at her sharply, and notice she's wearing a tiny smile.

"What are you even talking about?"

She nods her head to the right, and I follow the direction to find Aiden, Ben, and Owen talking on the other side of the hall. For some reason, even this far away, I feel like his attention is on me.

"That boy is jealous," Jade whispers just as Noel reaches us. "Hi Noel. Bye Noel." And just like that, I'm left looking after her.

"What was that about?" Noel asks as he watches Jade retreat.

"Just some girl stuff."

"That's kind of what I wanted to talk to you about."

That captures my attention, and I swing my eyes back to him. He's wearing that a little unsure expression of his, and I narrow my eyes.

"You wanted to talk about girl stuff?"

"Yes. No. Could we go somewhere?"

The moment he asks, my eyes dart to Aiden, who stands facing us, but his eyes are on the person in front of him. Yet, I have no doubt his attention is on me, if only by the rigid set of his shoulders. He usually only looks that frustrated when I'm involved. So, I decide to test Jade's theory.

"Sure!" I reply brightly before I tuck my arm through Noel's elbow. Out of the corner of my eye, I see Aiden's eyes dart toward us, and I suppress a smile. Maybe there is something to Jade's knowledge of boys. I don't read into it too much though, because I know just how territorial shifters can be. Sometimes it has nothing to do with the person in question. Just an alpha being an alpha. But pushing Aiden's buttons? That's something I do seem to enjoy.

"So, what's up?" I ask as soon as Noel and I are outside. There are a few benches set up, covered by the trees, but we don't head there. We walk down the tree path for a few minutes before Noel finally speaks up.

"I wanted to talk to you about the dance."

"Okay?"

"We're friends, right?"

"Of course."

"And I can talk to you about anything?"

"Yes." I'm not sure where this is going, but I really hope it has something to do with Jade and not him suddenly developing feelings for me. I've heard of stuff like that happening. Not that it would actually ever happen to me, but I like Noel, and I don't want things to be awkward between us.

"Well—" he stops again, and the suspense is killing me.

"Noel, just tell me."

"I like Jade," he blurts out before getting that embarrassed look all over his face. "I know you know. And I asked you to the dance, and I wouldn't have wanted to go with anyone else, but I don't want things to be weird between us because we got... I don't know... while dancing and I wanted to tell you because I like her and maybe nothing will happen between us, but I can't bear the thought of you and me not being friends either and..."

"Noel, take a breath!" I take him by the arms, giving him a little squeeze. "It's okay."

"You're not mad? Or... disappointed?"

"You mean heartbroken?" I give him a quick smile as he shifts uncomfortably from side to side. "No. We kind of had this conversation already, remember? Nothing changed. Even though you're an incredible dancer. And honestly, I like you for her. Not that I would push the issue," I hurry on to add, because I'm not about to start playing matchmaker. "But there're no hard feelings between us."

"Oh good," he says right before he grabs me in a hug. I give it back to him because I feel like I need it too. He really has become one of my closest friends, and I'm glad we are both on the same page.

"You've made me very happy, Maddie Hawthorne," Noel says, looking down at me. Before I can reply, someone clears his throat, and we turn to find Aiden standing a few feet away. I have no idea how long he's been there, but he for sure saw our hug and heard Noel just now. If the hard look in his eyes is any indication.

"Sorry to interrupt, but Headmaster Marković has sent me to fetch you. He would like a word." Then without a word, he turns on his heels and walks away.

"What is with Aiden lately?" Noel asks, looking at his

retreating figure. I shake my head, unsure of which answer I'd like to offer, settling on none.

"I better go," I say instead, and Noel nods.

"You're a great friend, Maddie."

"Right back at ya, Noel."

And just like that, we've cleared the air, and I honestly feel better. A part of me wondered if something would come from our little date and that moment on the dance floor, but after the dust settled, I couldn't see it. I'm glad Noel feels the same. I hurry toward the school and see that Aiden is waiting at the entrance. When I reach him, he doesn't speak but leads the way inside and toward the headmaster's office. I want to say something, but I can't figure out if this is a mood I can deal with right now. He's becoming more closed off and that's difficult to get past.

We reach the office and he knocks once before receiving an invitation. He pulls the door open, and I step inside. Then, before I can thank him, the door shuts and I'm all alone.

☙❧

WELL, NOT ENTIRELY ALONE, SINCE HEADMASTER MARKOVIĆ IS sitting at his desk. He stands when I enter, giving me a comforting smile.

"Come on in, Miss Hawthorne. Take a seat."

I do as I'm told, taking the chair on the left of the desk. Once I'm situated, headmaster resumes his place as well, always the gentlemen. It's honestly something my dad still does, and it makes me smile every time. He always waits for Mama and the rest of us to be seated at the dinner table before he takes his turn. The pain is sharp and quick, but this time I welcome it with the sweet memory.

"I'm sure you know why you're here," Headmaster Marković begins, and I shake my head.

"I have no idea, sir," I reply honestly, because at this point it could be all kinds of things.

"What happened Friday was a very unfortunate incident," he says, and of course. I should've expected them to get to me eventually. "Mr. Lawson told me what happened, but I would like to hear your side of the story. It may yield a clue."

"I'm not sure how helpful I can be, but I can tell you what I know."

He motions for me to go ahead, listening carefully. It doesn't take long to go over the details, and he nods his head throughout, as if this is much of what he heard from Aiden. Obviously, I leave out my own confusing feelings when it comes to the shifter, but I don't downplay his role in keeping me safe. I wouldn't have made it without him.

"Aiden is a capable young man," the headmaster comments when I tell him as much. "He will be a great leader one day."

"Leader?" I ask, a little desperate to know more about the boy who's been haunting my every thought for days. "Isn't the term usually alpha?"

"You are correct, but Mr. Lawson's situation is a bit unconventional."

"What does that mean?"

"I am not at liberty to discuss, I'm afraid." Just like that, that discussion is over, but I am left with so many more questions. "Let us focus back on the events of Friday night. I understand that you and your sisters had quite a run in with the Ancients two months ago."

"I don't see how that's relevant," I say before I can stop myself.

"It is because I do not want you to put yourself in any unnecessary danger just because you have... experience with battle magic "

Ah, I see. He thinks I'm out here looking for trouble. I can understand the misconception, to a point. The whole school thinks I'm some kind of a super witch or an adrenaline junkie. Not that anyone would actually say anything to my face, but I'm not blind to the looks I'm still the recipient of when no one thinks I'm paying attention. It's only natural the rumors would get to the headmaster eventually.

"Sir, all I did on Friday was try and help. It backfired a little, considering I got stuck outside and had to come face to face with whatever that thing was. But I don't do this on purpose."

The tone in my voice must get to him because after a long pause, he finally nods. I'm not sure if he truly believes me, but he's giving it consideration. That much I can tell.

"Sir." I decide to push my luck a little and ask the hard questions. "Did the Ancients send in their minions? Did they actually get through the protective wards?"

At first, I think he's not going to answer me. Headmaster Marković is wearing that contemplative expression my dad sometimes gets. He is trying to decide if he's going to be honest or if he's going to try and protect me from the truth. In the end, he surprises me.

"They did not. The spell came from within the grounds, just like the last time. It was a very advanced glamour, coupled with a few offensive spells. A fascinating combination." Headmaster leans over his desk, looking me right in the eye. "I ask that you do not spread that around, as we are doing everything we can to insure your safety. But if you can think of anything from your dealings with the Ancients and their magic, please come to me directly."

And that is why he told me anything. He thinks I have an insight, just like my sisters do, about the Ancients. But at this point, I'm afraid I've already exhausted that particular avenue. What I need to do is get to the secret library. It's been days since I've been there, and the amount of knowledge that place holds can be of tremendous help. I think maybe now is the time to tell the headmaster about it, but when I open my mouth, no words come out. Whatever magic spell is keeping the library secret, it's a powerful one.

"I have one more question. What happens to the students who are outside the lockdown protocol?"

"You mean the time you ended up in the forest?"

"Yes, sir."

"The reason we have rooms as the place to go in case of the

emergency is because the building itself is enchanted from generations past. The rest of the campus is too, but the enchantments
are not as strong. It is unfortunate that you and a few others were
unable to find shelter, and we are actively looking for ways to
change that. One of the teachers found a protective amulet spell
that we are trying to amplify now."

I understand all that, but the truth is, even the teachers can't
protect us if this place overrun.

"What I ask, is that you do your best to follow the rules and
stay close to areas which serve as a fortress against these types of
situations."

There is so much I could say, but it would do me no use. I'm
still just a student, and even though the headmaster gave me a lot
more information than I assumed he would, he's not going to tell
me everything. So, I give him my word and I'm dismissed. When I
leave the office, I half expect Aiden to be waiting for me, but he's
not. Miss Cindy, the headmaster's assistant, gives me a soft smile
before getting back to the task on her desk.

I walk to my room alone, my mind mulling over what I learned
and what to do next. I will definitely need to try to get to the
library tonight. I've been putting it off for way too long. It doesn't
help that the students have been under an incredible amount of
scrutiny. We're watched more than usual, and I'm not exactly
complaining in the grand scheme of thing. If it helps weed out the
bad seeds, I'm all for it.

But another part of me is frustrated because I have no way of
figuring out how to get to the library unseen. I think back to the
way the door appeared to me when I touched it, when my blood
seeped into the wood. There are secrets within those walls that are
mine alone. I have no idea what it will take to finally unravel them,
but I need to at least try. My whole existence may depend on it.

❧ 19 ❧

Once the lights out announcement is made, Jade and I are under our covers almost immediately. Both of us, as I'm sure is the case with the rest of the school, haven't been sleeping well. Plus, she has an early study date with her group, since they're presenting in our Elemental Magic class. I haven't been given a group yet because Mrs. Roberts likes to only have one group present every month.

It's about twenty minutes before Jade is fast asleep. I can always tell when she's zonked out. She kind of unclenches her whole body and spreads out. Especially lately, with everything going on, we've been going to bed all wound up. Careful not to disturb her too much, I grab the leggings and hoodie I stuffed under my comforter earlier in the day and get dressed under the covers. After grabbing my boots, I head for the door.

Before I exit, I take out two necklaces, wrapping my hand around the three crystals and the tiny bottle at the same time. Malachite, smoky quartz, and black tourmaline are attached to one of the necklaces as a charm. All three of the crystals are powerful protection talismans, and I can really use some invisibility right now. The little plastic bottle on the other necklace is filled with cinnamon, and a tiny seashell, for hard protection. I close my eyes, concentrating on reaching my center, before I push the intention through my hand and into the charms. The magic flares up, tingling my skin before it settles over me. This isn't going to make me invisible to the eye, but it will help guide me, so that I can stay off everyone's radar. And it'll mask me from the shifters. At least that's the plan.

That is another area of expertise I'd like to add to my list, protection wards and spells. I'm hoping the library can help me glean some information on that as well. I don't ever want to feel as helpless as I was in that barn structure with Aiden. I couldn't do anything with my magic, and that makes me a very useless witch.

The school has been implementing nightly security check ups, but they're not locking us in our rooms, in case we need to get out. I've been studying the security patterns since they upped the amount of patrols, and I'm about to put into test just how well I have it figured out.

It's not exactly ideal that the greenhouse and the entrance to the library are on the opposite side of the school. The helpful aspect of this adventure is that the school has plenty of nooks and crannies for me to hide in. The moment I see a shadow move, I dart into one of the indents in the hall or behind a pillar. It's slow going, but I manage to stay off anyone's radar.

When I finally reach the greenhouse, I'm surprised no one is stationed outside. It would make sense to be on rotation every-where else, but this seems like a vulnerable entry point. Although, we've already discovered that we've got a wolf in sheep's clothing amongst us. Maybe it's pointless to try to keep someone from getting in when they're already here.

Once I'm inside the greenhouse, I do a quick scan but see and hear nothing. Satisfied that I'm alone, I move toward the far corner and the crates stacked there. A part of me is nervous at how easy it was to come down here, across the whole school. And how easy it would be for someone to hide right under our noses. They only need to know a little bit about their magic to create spells and charms. Nothing huge though because the school monitors magic activity. But something little, like the magic I created, it's mostly about intention. It can go unnoticed pretty easily. Not to mention, if the Ancients are supplying any of the spells or the magic, it would be nearly untraceable since it's not a signature the school has seen before.

Great, I just proved to myself that it can literally be anyone in this school. I'm not sure how that makes me feel. However, as I move the crates aside and the familiar rug greets me, I smile. This place, the library, it makes me feel like I'm not useless. Like I can do something. I haven't talked to my family all week, and I try very hard not to think just how much I wish I could. But I understand the precautions needed to keep the communication to a minimum. Still, I'm doing nothing to help find my father, and I'm doing nothing to help this school. All that is about to change.

I move the rug aside, pulling at the door in the next motion. The stale air of the underground greets me, but it doesn't take away from the excitement I'm feeling. I need this. I'm about to step down when a noise reaches my ears. I spin around, searching through the darkness and the plants, when I see a glow behind the row of greenery. My heart leaps into my throat, and my battle magic awakens. But even so, I don't run. Something keeps me rooted to that spot.

When the wolf walks out of the aisle, I realize it's because some crazy part of me knew it was Aiden. I can't tell if it's the feel of him in the air around me, or the look in his eyes. Even in wolf form, he's so purely Aiden.

The wolf walks toward me, stopping just a few feet away as we study each other. I've seen him before, when he came to get me in the woods, but this seems different. It seems more intimate some-how. As if he comes to some conclusion, he steps behind a row of plants, and then he's Aiden again. His eyes find me in the darkness once more, his bare chest a sight to behold. He reaches behind the plants and pulls out a pair of pants before he puts them on. A sweater comes next, but I just stand there, mesmerized as I watch him dress. I have no desire to run and hide. We're about to have a conversation, and I'm going to have to trust him completely. Something I'm really not good at.

When he finally steps out from behind the bushes that so strategically hid most of him from me, he's dressed. And his eyes are once again on me.

"Well, Duchess. You just can't keep yourself away from trouble."

⊙✺⊙

"I AM ABSOLUTELY NOT GETTING INTO TROUBLE," I FEEL inclined to point out when he's standing just two feet away from me. He glances down at the open hole in the ground, before meeting my eyes once again. "This is not trouble."

"Really? Sneaking out of your room in the middle of the night and then unearthing some walkway into the underground is not trouble?"

"Nope. I'm just minding my Ps and Qs." I shrug, and surprisingly, that earns me a tiny grunt that almost sounds like a chuckle. I resist the urge to smile. Sometimes it's very easy to forget that Aiden and I are not friends.

"You are the only girl I know who's got the idiom collection of an elderly man."

"Why thank you, Aiden Lawson. You really know how to compliment a girl." I cross my arms in front of me, giving him the sweetest look I can manage. He smirks at me, but I still count this as a victory. If I can get under his skin even a fraction of how he gets under mine, it's points on my board. But all this back and forth is only stalling. We both know we have to talk about the entryway behind me.

At that moment, a noise reaches us, and Aiden steps forward, taking my arm and pulling me down beside him. My skin tingles under his hold, and I try not to let that become a visibly physical reaction. He looks over at me, our faces just a few inches apart, and for a moment, we're suspended in time. Just the two of us, breathing in the same air. Then, the sound of footsteps reaches us, and Aiden narrows his eyes, as if telling me to stay put. I nod, and then the pressure on my arm is gone and he's standing up.

"Hey, Pete," Aiden calls out as he disappears from view. "What's up?"

"Nothing much. Just thought I'd get some fresh air."

"Sorry man, but Headmaster said to keep the doors locked," Aiden replies, moving farther away from where I'm crouching down.

"Ugh, these patrols are killing me. I need to be in those woods," Pete replies. I can't see him, but for some reason I think he's the blonde guy Aiden hangs out with. He's not in any of my classes, so I can't be sure, but I believe he's a year ahead of us.

"I get it, trust me I do. I'll see if I can arrange something soon, alright?"

A few more words are exchanged, but they moved farther away, and I can't quite make them out. I think they're inside the school now, but I still don't move. Aiden is doing me a serious solid by keeping my secret. He's going to want answers in return. A part of me wants to climb down into the catacombs and hide away, but he would just come after me. Aiden isn't exactly one to give up.

After what seems like an hour, he finally comes back. I've settled right down on the floor, since my legs have gone to sleep crouching. He gives me an amused look, before he offers me his hand. I look at it like it's a snake that might bite me, but for some reason, I still accept it and let him pull me up to standing position.

"Are you going to take me on an excursion now?" he asks, his lips curling up at the corners. I roll my eyes, but I really have no choice.

"Look, where I'm going, it's a secret. But not because it's some-thing bad," I hurry on to add. "It's something I..." There it goes not letting me finish explaining. I huff, before I continue. "If I show you, you have to promise not to say anything." Not that he will have much chance, but I feel like I need this from him before we can go any farther.

"I don't—"

"Promise," I interrupt, looking into his eyes intently. I'm never sure what he sees when he looks at me, but right now, it feels like we're on the same wavelength. The intensity behind his gaze always makes me a bit unbalanced, but right now, it almost adds fuel to my fire. After a moment he seems to realize just how important this is to me, and he nods.

"Out loud." I don't even think when I say the words, but it's something dad used to always say. It means more if the promise is spoken out loud. As if a verbal contract has been made. The emotion almost chokes me, but I push it down. I think Aiden sees it anyway but doesn't comment. He seems to be able to understand my moods better than I do at times.

"I promise."

Just two words, but they mean the world to me. There is no doubt he means them, if the way he's looking at me is any indication. We've taken a few more steps forward. I hope he doesn't take twice as many back.

"We have to cover this up, so no one finds it while we're gone." I point to the plants I usually stack in front of the entrance. "You go first, and I'll follow."

He doesn't question, trusting me, which is surprising all on its own. I wait for him to descend, as I move the plants in their designated spots. Then, I place the rug over the door and pull both over me as I close it. Even though we're in complete darkness, I know my way well enough. Aiden's arms reach for me when I'm close to the bottom, wrapping around my waist. I don't need his help, but I appreciate the gesture. Even so, I don't pull away. I allow him to guide me to the ground before I kneel and grab the flashlights I left here previously.

"Ready?" I ask, as I click on the light. He's standing right in front of me, his eyes doing a quick study of the tunnel. I push the other flashlight at him and move past before I do something stupid and ask if I can have a hug. The desire is sudden and nearly overwhelming, and I squash it down.

I'm becoming mush around him, and that is not allowed.

𝒮𝓁 20 𝒮𝓁

When we reach the spot where the door should be, it's not. I can tell Aiden is skeptical, but this is just part of what makes this library so special. It only reveals itself to me.

I step forward, placing my hand against the dark wall. At first, nothing happens. But then, the dirt ripples under my skin, and the door slowly appears, as if floating up to the top. Aiden inhales sharply, and I grin without turning around. I can't exactly credit this awesome magic to only myself, but the fact that it answers to me is pretty incredible. A part of me is excited to share this with someone. And yes, excited that the someone is Aiden. Even though I'm trying very hard not to let that become a thing.

When we step inside, I let Aiden through, watching his face for a reaction. His eyes scan over every surface, taking it all in at once. I close the door and follow him deeper into the library as the little hallway ends and the space opens up into the large high-ceilinged circular room.

"What is this place?" Aiden asks, his voice full of awe. It gives me a twinge of pride, seeing him amazed at this space just like I was. Like I still am.

"A library like no other. There are volumes upon volumes of ancient texts I've never even heard of. It's how I found the spell that helped my sisters."

He turns at that, his eyes on me. "You've known about this place that long? Why haven't you said anything?"

"Honestly, I'm not sure. I tried to tell the headmaster a few times last year, but I think there's a spell that prevents me to do so. The place opened up to me that first time when I touched it with some of my blood. It's like it's only meant for me. I can't explain it. It's just a feeling I have."

I think he'll try to play it off or tell me how stupid that feeling is since this could be a huge help if it truly holds all these treasures, but he does neither. He turns back to the room and does another scan before he nods.

"I understand," he says before he walks toward the large window. My heart fills with just those two words, and I'm glad he's not looking at me. I'm sure my face will betray everything I'm feeling.

Seeing him here, a place that's so uniquely mine I think it holds a piece of me within it, I can't seem to keep my emotions in check. He continues to walk around, mesmerized by the sheer volume of this place. The wonder in his eyes is the same one I felt when I stepped inside the first time, and he's not hiding it from me. For this one moment, he's letting me see a real emotion in him, and I hold onto that. I have a feeling I'll be cherishing it down the line, long after this is all over.

"How many of these books have you studied?" Aiden's voice reaches out to me, and I realize I've been gawking at him. Shaking myself a little, I head for the table I've been using as my base of operation, a few dozen books piled on its surface.

"Not very many. It's difficult to sneak over here, as you can imagine." As I take a seat, Aiden comes around, taking the one next to me.

"You really haven't told anyone of this place?"

"Last year, when I first stumbled upon it, my best friend Kate was here. I brought her in, and she helped a lot. Also, Liam. He's a Fae. He didn't come back this semester, but he helped me decipher the spell that helped my sisters. Some of the books here are in different languages and from different realms."

"That's fascinating." Aiden turns, staring out the window at the evergreen forest. The light is just right, as always, making it seem like it's late afternoon and not the middle of the night. "And what's out there?"

"I've never been able to discover that," I say, looking out the window myself. "It always looks the same, the forest and the time of the day. There are no doors leading out that way and honestly, a part of me likes the mystery. I'm afraid it would be something disappointing."

I'm not sure what possesses me to add that last part, it's a little too intimate for us, but once again, Aiden doesn't make fun of me. He nods, as if he understands, and we share a look that sears me to my very core. Time seems to stop as we watch each other, and I think something shifts again, putting us into a new category. Too bad I have no idea what that means for us.

Tearing my gaze away, I grab for the first book on the table and pull it toward me. I need to concentrate. This is why I'm here. To check for protection spells, and to see if there's anything here to help us find the traitor.

"What can I do to help?"

"Grab a book and see what you can find," I reply, barely sparing him a glance. I can't let myself get distracted again. "There's no index or an organized system. Sometimes books appear where I didn't leave them, but that's very rare. One day, I think I want to spend time in here just to create some kind of organization to the chaos. But for now, I just read. And take notes."

When I glance up, Aiden is watching me once more. He grabs the first book in front of him and flashes me the tiniest of smiles,

"Read I can do."

I think my whole world shifts with that one look. I don't ever remember seeing him smile, and even though it's not a full one, it's the closest I've gotten, and it makes all the difference. There's a lightness in Aiden I haven't seen before, and I have no idea if it's this place or my sharing it with him, but I hold onto this moment and the memory it's creating.

It's a bit of simple peace in a world gone completely crazy.

THE NEXT MORNING, I CAN HARDLY CONCENTRATE. I HAVE A million thoughts in my mind and none of them are anything I can share with Jade or any of my other friends. And even though Aiden is in the know about the library, part of what I want to discuss has to do with him. All I want is to talk to my sisters.

"What has gotten into you today? Jade asks, as we head toward the dining room later in the day.

"I just asked her this," Vera comments, coming up to the other side of me. She had to repeat the question too because I was so lost in thought I didn't even realize she was talking to me.

"Sorry." I give both of them a quick smile as we reach the dining room and get in line. "I just have a lot to think about."

"Like what?" Christy jumps in, materializing beside us. I resist the urge to roll my eyes, but her nosiness is not appreciated right now.

"Just missing my family," I decide on a half-truth, but it seems to be enough. The girls all get a faraway look in their eyes, their own homesickness making an appearance. If they can relate to anything, it's missing our families. The lockdown hasn't been easy on anyone. I saw a few students coming out of the headmaster's office just yesterday, wiping tears from their eyes.

"I know what we should do!" Christy exclaims, clapping her hands with excitement effectively breaking the silence. "We should have a slumber party."

Not that she would know this, but her words bring a bigger

bout of sadness. I've only ever had a slumber party with my sisters. Even Kate and I never had a designated slumber party. That ping of awareness resonates in my chest, and I blink away unwanted tears. I'm not about to become a blabbering crying mess in the middle of the dining hall.

When I'm busy, it's so easy to forget how far away I am from family. But in times like these, I feel it in my very being.

"We can have it in Jade and Maddie's room. We can get a bunch of snacks and talk and braid hair..."

Christy's enthusiasm may be little over the top for my grumpy heart at times, but it can also be contagious. Even though the idea is appealing, it would put a damper on my plans. There is no way I'd be able to sneak away to the library. And as I keep reminding myself, that's my priority at the moment. But it's not like I can tell them that part.

"Yes! Let's do it, Maddie!" Jade chimes in, and now I'm between a rock and a hard place. I turn to the last girl in our group, hoping Vera's antisocial nature will save me from this impromptu party but no dice.

"Let's," is all she says, shrugging, as she reaches for an apple. This counts as her stamp of approval, and now I'm really stuck.

"Yes, yes!" Christy squeaks, earning a few looks thrown her way, but she doesn't care. "I will absolutely organize everything and get permission, and this will be great!"

"What will?" Noel asks, coming up to the group and reaching past me to grab a carton of orange juice. He flashes me a warm smile, stopping beside me.

"Is that all you're getting?" I ask, nodding toward his juice.

"I already grabbed food." He motions toward the table, and a few of his friends sitting beside a tray full of food. "I'm a growing boy. There is no way I'd be able to function on this little juice box."

I chuckle, which earns me another smile, before we all head toward the said table. Noel and I have really reached a new level in our friendship after our talk. There's a comfortable camaraderie between us that's almost thrilling.

When I went home in the summer to help my sisters, my whole town had a different kind of a dynamic. Shifters and witches were working together like they've been doing it all their lives. And more so, my sisters had guys in the house. For dinner. And movie night. Normal stuff.

It was new and fascinating.

I grew up in a community that is consciously female, and I've never thought anything of it. I love my coven and wouldn't trade it for anything. But besides Nolan's brother, I've never had many guy friends. When Liam stayed in Faery with his family instead of coming back this semester, I was once again minus guy friendships.

But here is Noel, someone I'm starting to trust. It's a new experience for me, and not one I'm complaining about. Maybe one of these days I'll be comfortable enough to ask him about Aiden. But not yet.

Christy is still chattering about the party, and while Jade and I have already exchanged a few looks, it's too late to bail now. I watch the petite brunette, amazed at her energy and go-get-them attitude. I think even if we resisted, she would've gotten her way. Maybe I need a little more of that in my life.

As I sit there, and let the conversation flow around me, a tingle starts up at the back of my spine, and I raise my eyes to scan my surroundings. Almost immediately my gaze lands on Aiden who has just walked into the room. He finds me right away, as if drawn to me, but doesn't approach. Talk about a new experience. What's happening between Aiden and me is even more unlike anything in my life before.

I find myself falling deeper and deeper under his spell. Noel bumps me with his shoulder, and I look over to see him pointing to the pepper he can't reach. I pass it on and when I look back at Aiden he is already lost in the crowd.

Glancing back at Noel, I wonder why can't I be attracted to someone like him? I know he's crushing on Jade, but he's got plenty of nice friends I'm sure he would be happy to set me up with. But no. Instead I'm getting all twisted up inside over tall, dark, and broody. I'm not sure how I'm supposed to spend my nights in the library with him.

Which brings me back to my initial dilemma. I look over at Christy one more time. I need to take a page out of her book and light some fires. Maybe if I'm even half as persistent as Christy, the headmaster will let me talk to my family.

❧ 21 ❧

After lunch, I wave goodbye to my friends and head straight toward the headmaster's office. I'm done with classes for the day, and I don't have training with Aiden for another couple of hours. I'm prepared to sit outside and wait Headmaster Marković out if need be. But when I reach the office, he's talking to Miss Cindy, and when I ask if I can speak to him, he makes time for me right away.

"What can I help you with, Miss Hawthorne?" he asks, motioning to the chair in front of his desk I occupied last time.

Deciding that diving right in is my best bet, I sit up straighter, leaning my shoulders back and meeting the headmaster's gaze head on.

"I need to speak with my sisters."

His eyes flash with something that is gone before I can identify it. He leans back in his chair, studying me carefully.

"Now, Miss Hawthorne, you know we are under strict rules at the moment."

"I understand that, Headmaster." I dare to interrupt, growing bolder by the minute. This is family, and that fuels me like nothing else. "But I ask you to give me this one leeway. It's been too long

136

since I've heard from them and with my father still missing... I'm sure you can understand how unsettling that can be."

Even though we both know what I'm doing is manipulative, I think Headmaster is a little proud of me for speaking up. I'm typically the one to keep to the background. I've always found it easier, since I have such powerful sisters. I don't have to be the one in the spotlight. It's why I hate it so much. But even if he's not proud of me, I am. It seems I'm finally finding my footing, and I'm not about to back down now.

"This is not to become a habit." The headmaster surprises me. "If I allow direct communication, it cannot be more than fifteen minutes."

"Understood," I reply, trying to keep the excitement at bay. But my whole body is buzzing with the prospect of hearing my sister's voices. If I get extra lucky, my mom might be there too. But I know that's less likely at the moment, so I will take what I can get.

Headmaster Marković pulls out a drawer before producing an older rotary phone. All of our cell phones were confiscated when the school went on lockdown, so even this piece of communication technology makes me happy. He proceeds to wave his hand over the device, and I can feel the magic stir in the air before he mumbles a few words under his breath.

"You have fifteen minutes, Miss Hawthorne." Headmaster Marković motions toward the phone before standing and walking out of the room. I don't waste a second to grab the receiver, dialing my house number. As the last rotation falls into place, I listen to the ringing in my ear, hoping my sisters are home by now. Unless something happened, at least one of them should be home.

After what seems like a hundred rings, no one answers. I push the hook down on the phone and dial Bri's shop next. If they're not at home, at least Bri should be at the store.

"Herbs & Trinkets, how can I help you?" Harper's voice sounds on the line, and I breathe a sigh of relief.

"Finally! Why aren't you home?"

"Maddie?!" Harper exclaims, and then I hear some commotion in the background, and Bri's voice comes on the line.

"Maddie, is something wrong?"

I realize after weeks of very strict communication rules, I probably just freaked them out.

"I'm okay, I promise. I managed to talk Headmaster Marković into letting me speak with you," I hurry on to say, and I can almost hear my sisters' shoulders relax.

"If you called, then you're not entirely okay," Harper comments gently, and I grin despite myself. They know me too well.

"I just miss you is all. Are there any news of dad?"

The silence on the other end of the line is heavy, and I know the answer before they even say it.

"No. Mama is with the council, trying to see if we can find another tracing spell," Harper replies, and I nod, even though they can't see me. It makes sense, but I wish Mom was there so I could hear her voice as well.

"What is it, Maddie?" Bri ask, her older sister senses tingling.

"There's just a lot going on," I begin, unsure of exactly to approach the subject. Even though Headmaster is giving me privacy, I doubt he's going to be too keen on me sharing sensitive information. Even though I know he enchanted the phone before he let me use it.

"I'm trying to find more information in that... place I told you about." This secrecy spell is really getting in the way of my communication. I have got to find a way around it.

"The... place." Bri stops, clearly confused. "Why can't I name it?"

"I think it's an enchantment. To keep it extra safe. I can't say it either, and when I've tried telling Headmaster about it, my mouth just won't work."

"That's curious," Harper comments, and I understand what she means. "I would be interested to know the reason behind it, if you ever do figure it out."

"I will," I can't believe after all this time I'm finally talking to my sisters. "But how is everything? Is everyone okay?"

"We are, Mads," Harper says. "The spell is holding strong for now, and it's been a very quiet month. If we stay inside the barrier."

"And the outside?"

"We try not to worry about that for now," Bri hurries to say, and that tells me what I need to know. A lot more is going on than they want to tell me. We're still protecting each other, even across miles and miles of distance. "But what about you? How are you? We miss you."

"I'm okay," I reply, wondering how much to tell them and how much they may already know. "This place has had its share of adventures, that's for sure. But I'm holding my own."

"Of course you are."

"There's also a boy," I say before I can stop myself. My sisters inhale simultaneously, making me laugh. "It's not unheard of."

"Tell us about him."

I think of how best to describe Aiden, and after a moment, all I can come up with is, "He's frustrating."

"Ah, those are the best kind," Bri replies, and I smile at the dreamy tone of her voice. From what she told me, she and Mark didn't exactly see eye to eye in the beginning.

"It's not like that. Well, I actually don't know. He's been training me in combat. And he knows about the place. He seems to be everywhere, and I just don't know what to do about it." The words rush out of me at once, as if I've been holding them in this whole time.

"Maddie, boys have a tendency to mess with our minds. And they don't even have to do much. It's kind of part of their DNA makeup."

"So, I'm supposed to be confused?"

"It's part of the process, I'm afraid," Harper comments and tears come to my eyes unbidden. I wish they were here. I wish I could sit and talk to them face to face.

"You'll figure out how you feel, Maddie," Bri says. "You are a smart girl. Even when he's driving you crazy, don't forget that. It's easy to let feelings cloud our judgement. But also, don't run from them. It's okay to embrace them and use them as tools to help guide you. We're emotional creatures by nature. But just because we are, doesn't mean we're not strong and resilient. You're a Hawthorne. That boy better watch out."

But running from my feelings is what I'm good at apparently. I've been denying it for weeks now, the pull I feel toward him. And a part of me has no idea what to do with this information.

"Thanks," I say, instead of getting into the details. I feel like I'm almost out of time. "I'll keep digging on my end, and please keep me updated. I feel so disconnected being this far away."

"We miss you, Mads. But you're always in our thoughts," Bri says warmly, and I tuck her words deep inside of me.

Just then, the door opens, and Headmaster Marković steps back into the room. My time is up.

"I love you," I add hurriedly.

"Love you too," my sisters echo, and then the line dies.

⚜

INSTEAD OF HEADING BACK TO MY ROOM AFTER MY TALK, I GO outside. The weather has been turning cooler by the day, but I don't grab a jacket.

I follow the avenue of limes as it curves around the fountain and toward the pond. But rather than moving toward the little island, I keep going.

Kate and I explored some of the grounds last year, but we weren't as brave as I'm feeling right now. When everything started happening with the Ancients, everyone got paranoid. We were pretty confined to the main building for half of the year. Kate hated it. Her family is way stricter than mine, and she longed for the school to be her freedom. But now she's back home, and I have no idea how she's dealing. Not that her family is terrible or anything. They just put a lot of pressure on her. Which I can now understand firsthand.

My parents have always allowed me to be my own self. Yes, they want me to be successful, but it has never been about putting unrealistic expectations on me. I mostly do that to myself. But since the battle in Hawthorne, since I returned for my third semester, it's like everyone around me is holding me to that unreachable standard. Even the headmaster succumbed to it by letting me use the phone when no one else can. They're all expecting me to be something great. I'm not sure I'm cut out for that kind of greatness.

I'm good at magic, and I'm good at research. I always envisioned myself more as a Watcher, like my dad, than a leader like my mom and sisters. But now I'm being put in all kinds of situations that require me to be the one at the front. Like the library. Why can't I tell the headmaster about it? Why is knowledge of the place so guarded? It feels like I'm being given this responsibly over all this information, and I have no idea what to do about it.

When the trees around me get thicker, I realize I've walked farther than I planned. I'm on the opposite side of the pond, as far away from the school as I've ever been, while still within the grounds. From where I am, the island in the "middle" of the pond seems to actually be much farther away. I see that it's not directly halfway between the two ends. This side of the pond is much wider, almost like its pear shaped. I'm not sure why it's even called a pond. It's large enough to be a lake. But then again, what do I know.

Walking up to the water, I squat down to let my hand run over the silky waves. The breeze is just strong enough to make the sparkling liquid dance. When my finger dips into the pond, my magic shudders within me, as if shaking itself awake.

Maybe this isn't the greatest idea, but the call is too loud to ignore. I glance around quickly, but the coast is clear. The chill of autumn has been creeping in for days now, and the water is going to be even colder, but I can't help myself.

Stripping down, I'm in my undergarments and a tank. The air moves around me, prickling my skin with goosebumps. Before I can think too much of it, I step right up to the bank and dive in headfirst. The shock almost makes me come back up, but then the water engulfs me entirely, and I feel safe. I swim for a few seconds, then finally break the surface. A few months ago, I met Skylar, the newest addition to my hometown. She's half mermaid shifter, half witch, so her body temperature regulates in water, unlike mine. But even so, I enjoy the chill of the liquid against me.

The feel of the drops racing down my skin sooth me like a familiar caress. Sure, I take showers every day and am surrounded by water, but this feels different. There's something freeing about the natural water around, water that's connected directly to the earth. My magic is going haywire inside of me, bursting to be set free, and after a few seconds, I let it.

Surprisingly though, it builds slowly, like an oncoming storm. First, the waves move around me as if barely touched by the wind. But then, the turbulence starts, and the small pond becomes an angry ocean. The wind dances around me, sending some of the water into a whirlpool right in front of my eyes. If I was anyone else, I might be terrified at this display of power. Storms can be unpredictable, but I don't fear this one. I embrace it.

Lying back onto my back, I allow myself to float as I spread my arms out, and with it my magic. I'm being taken on a ride, and all I want to do is get lost in it. I close my eyes, and feel the magic pulse through me while the waves beat at my skin.

Suddenly, a pair of arms wrap around my waist, yanking me upright. Instead of screaming in surprise, I react. My leg comes up hard, my knee connecting with my attacker. My magic almost solidifies the water beneath me, and instead of trying to retreat, I'm suspended in place as I unleash my magic. I push both of my palms out, slamming them directly into the hard chest. The move and my magic blasts into the attacker, sending him skidding across the top of the water. At the last moment, before I plunge him into the depths beneath, I realize it's Aiden.

"Are you out of your freaking mind?" I scream dropping my hands and retracting my magic. Aiden drops below the surface of the water but comes up for air in the next moment.

"Are you trying to get yourself killed?" he yells in response, pushing the hair out of his face. With water dripping down his skin and his hair in disarray, he looks ridiculously attractive. But also very mad.

"Excuse me? I should be asking you that!" Now that my magic knows I'm not in danger, it settles, but barely, still just under my skin. He swims a few feet over, his eyes on me as the storm continues to dance around us. It quiets enough that it's not a danger to us but doesn't dissipate completely.

"I thought you were in trouble," Aiden says, not taking his eyes off me. Whatever I am about to say dies on my lips. There's genuine concern in his voice and it pierces me right through. Just then, he must hear how he sounds because his eyes dart away from my face, and to the water around us. I tread it to move closer to him, and now we're only a few feet apart.

"We're in water, Aiden. That's kind of my thing. My magic, it needed some exercise." I shrug, and his eyes come back to my face. A huge part of me wants to close the distance between us and reach out. I'm not sure what I'm feeling yet, but I'm feeling it so intensely and entirely about Aiden.

"So, what you showed me in training, that wasn't even half of it?"

"No. Ever since the ritual I performed with my sisters, my magic has been unpredictable. For a while there, I thought it went dormant. But now I know it's been growing. Slowly."

"And you have been repressing it." He says it like a statement, but I still feel inclined to answer it like a question.

"Repressing it is easier than trying to explain it to the headmaster. I'm already too visible for my liking."

"You don't have to hide around me," he says it so quietly, but since it's just the two of us, I hear him. Not only that, I feel every word deep inside. My eyes catch onto his and suddenly, I want to show him what I can do.

"If I use too much magic, they'll be able to tell," I say, still watching him as I swim a little closer. "You need to be closer."

His eyes flash at my words, but then he swims toward me, so there's nothing but a sliver of water and my tank between us. If I breathe too deeply, our chests will brush against each other.

"I have to touch you." I realize how it sounds the moment I say it, but Aiden doesn't blink, just nods, giving me permission. One of my hands falls to my side, as my magic trickles down beneath our feet, while my other arm traces up Aiden's shoulder. It comes to rest right at the nape of his neck, and suddenly, we're breathing the same air.

The feel of him under my fingertips warms me from the inside, and the water doesn't feel so cold anymore. Aiden jerks, glancing down, trying to see through the water as the liquid solidifies to let us stand in one place. His hands drop to my waist, since he no longer has to tread water, and now I'm flush against him.

"Did you freeze it?" he whispers, rearranging our bodies a little.

"No. Kind of just packed the water molecules into something more solid than not." It's the best explanation I can come up with but it's enough. He looks fascinated. "If it gets too much, hold tight."

It's the only warning I give him as I raise the hand I've had in the water straight over our heads. The water rises all around us, creating a wall way over ten feet tall. Instead of keeping them straight, I pull at the points at the top and begin twisting them together. The waves and the wind dance, creating a beautiful picture, with us smack dab in the middle of it.

"It's like a Hershey's kiss," Aiden whispers in awe, staring straight up to where the funnel is twisting. I grin at his description, because I can see it. The waves move around us restlessly, and we're pushed even closer together. Our noses bump and everything inside of me stills. Aiden's hands flex on my hips, his whole body rigid, and it's like he's holding himself frozen to the spot. The storm around us is the same storm I see in his eyes. My breathing shallows as I try to swallow, but even with all this water, I'm ridiculously thirsty. His eyes flash again, and it's like he can see right into my head. All I have to do is move half an inch and his lips would be on mine. I've never been kissed, and I want him to be the first.

A gust of wind comes out of nowhere, pushing the water over us, and I tear my eyes away from Aiden to watch my magic spin completely out of control. Just for a moment, it's ruled by my emotions, and it's become unstable. The delicate way it was twining together has now become completely unbalanced. I try to pull it in, and I know what will happen when I do.

"Take a deep breath," I command, before it all comes crashing down on us.

22

"Are you okay?" Aiden asks as we pull ourselves out of the water and onto the bank. We're both breathing heavily, soaking wet, and I have no idea how to answer that question. I nod, before I collapse onto my back, staring up at the sky.

Was I really just thinking about kissing Aiden? Did I really let my magic get out of control because I allowed myself to focus on him? This pull, this need I feel towards him, it's terrifying and exhilarating at the same time.

But the logical part of me understands that if he felt anything toward me, he would've taken the opening. Wouldn't he? Maybe that's something I need to talk to Jade about. She's at least has had a boyfriend before. While she might be clueless at times, she definitely knows more than I do. But for now, I'll just lay here, feeling embarrassed. Which is when I realize I'm still near naked, and he's only a few feet away.

"Maddie—" Aiden begins, but I can't meet his eye. Almost blindly, I reach for my shirt, pulling it over my head. I contemplate hiding behind the material, but I don't need to look any dumber than I already do.

"Maddie." This time his voice is a lot closer, and when my head pops out of the collar, I realize he's moved to stand beside me. I'm still sitting down, so I have to look way up to see his face. Which I don't. I reach for my pants next, pulling them over my legs in the most awkward way possible. My clothes soak through, and I shake my head at myself. Closing my eyes for a second, I pull on the water covering my body, flickering it away. Just like that, I'm dry again.

"Neat trick," Aiden comments as I stand. He's still shirtless, but I see that he didn't take his jeans off before jumping in. He was clearly worried about me, and I try to keep my heart from reacting to that.

"Stay still," I say, before I focus on the water clinging to him. It's hard not to stare at his magnificent chest, but I manage, just barely. "All done."

"Thanks."

I move away, as he pulls his sweater over his head, giving me a second to collect my thoughts. I need to stop letting my emotions rule my actions. Aiden and I are not friends. He's told me we would never be friends. I don't know why I would assume or hope we could ever be anything more.

"Do you want to train right now?" he surprises me by asking. I expected him to leave right away. He seems like he wants to.

"Sure," I reply, dropping my sweater before I can put it back on. Aiden takes his stance in front of me, and I follow suit. We've never trained outside before, and the feel of nature all around us exhilarates me. At my core, I am an elemental witch, after all. The more connected I am to the elements, the stronger I feel. And being this close to the water, with the droplets still clinging to the grass under our feet, I feel almost invincible.

Yet, when I raise my head and meet Aiden's steady gaze, all kinds of other emotions rush in. The magic didn't completely dry off his hair, and the water glimmers, clinging to his dark locks. I fight the sudden urge to reach over and send them into disarray with my fingers.

Now that I know what his skin feels like under my fingertips, it's difficult to focus on anything else. He's wearing a shirt once again, but it's almost as if I can see right through it.

"You ready?" Aiden's voice snaps me out of my thoughts. My face heats up, and I duck my head as I nod.

Aiden doesn't hesitate to attack. He moves toward me in one fluid motion, his right arm swinging at my neck. I block automatically, now so attuned to his movements, it's like a dance. My mind goes blank, focusing entirely on the way his body shifts with mine. Somewhere in the last month, we may not have become friends, but we have become partners.

I notice his move just a fraction before he sweeps his leg around. But it's enough for me to throw my body on him instead of falling down to my side like he intended. I wrap my legs around his middle, allowing my whole body to lean into the motion and then we're falling. At the last moment, he cradles me against him, and I unwrap my legs, so as not to get squished. He ends up beneath me, with me straddling his stomach, my head in the crook of his neck. For just a second we lay like this, breathing heavily as we both try to find stability in a world gone mad.

When I finally pull back, my hair falls over my shoulder, barely grazing his neck. His arm comes up, pushing the locks behind my ear and the movement is so tender, it brings tears to my eyes. Once more, we're in this moment of indecision. I want to lean down, and I want him to lean forward and neither one of us moves. His eyes grow dark, and his body tenses beneath mine, and then in one move, he's on his feet and he's setting me on mine.

"You're getting better," Aiden says, before he grabs his discarded shoes and leaves me standing beside the water. The compliment is so unusual that I don't get a chance to reply.

What is happening? I watch his retreating back, until he disappears. That's when I realize he didn't head toward the school. He went into the forest. A part of me wants to race after him, but I know that would be foolish. I've done enough foolish things for one day.

I sit back down on the grass, pulling on my own shoes. My

body feels recharged after being in the water, and even that small spar didn't exhaust me like it usually does. Or maybe I really am getting better.

It seems that no matter what I do, I end up with more questions. Talking to my family helped, but it also made me miss them that much more. I can't think about my father without a part of me shriveling up inside. And now, Aiden is a puzzle I can't seem to solve. I'm not sure I'm cut out for all this, but it's not as if I have a choice.

Yet for this one moment, I stay by the water, and watch it dance in the tiny breeze in front of me, soothing my aching heart with its magic.

֍

THE NEXT DAY, AIDEN IS GONE. WHEN I FINALLY GOT BACK TO my room, I went straight for homework, deciding to keep my weird feelings to myself. At least for now. Even though Jade and I haven't known each other for long, I trust her enough to talk to her about this. Just not yet.

I have to sort myself out before I can articulate what I'm feeling.

"Good news!" Christy runs up to me as I'm heading to potions class. "I got permission, and we're on for tonight!" She does her signature squeal, clapping her hands together and my heart drops a little. Apparently, a part of me was really hoping the faculty would advise her against this.

"We're on?" Jade asks, coming up to us. All four of us are in the class, and I'm sure Vera is already there. She doesn't dilly dally, but usually heads straight for her next class. I kind of like that about her. She's dependable. Whereas Christy is very... loud.

"We are absolutely on!" Another squeal. "I so cannot wait. It's going to be perfect. I'll grab snacks after lunch, since I don't have class. And after Jade's training, I can meet in your room and set it all up. I got a projector from the lab. Oh, and extra blankets."

149

We reach our class, and I'm thankful. My mood is definitely heavy on the grumpy because I have no excitement in me to be bothered with this sleepover. My eyes scan the hallway outside the room, and I internally berate myself because I'm looking for Aiden. He has a class across the way, but I don't see him.

"You okay?" Vera asks as I take a seat beside her. Even though Vera is a shifter, she has some witch blood in her, so she's been wanting to learn about our ways. I give her a quick nod, and she takes it at face value. Christy is still talking about the party, turned so she can face us. She and Jade are at the table in front of us.

Just when I'm about to put my head down in hopes of Christy taking it as a sign to lower her volume, the teacher walks in. Mrs. Housely always looks like she's ready to walk down a runaway. Today she has on a yellow skirt that hugs her hips and flares at the bottom, with a black and white blouse tucked into the waistline. A large belt sits across her stomach, matching her heels. She's got 50s chic style down, and I'm a little envious. I'd love to be able to pull something like that off. All in all, Mrs. Housely definitely breaks the mold when it comes to what one would expect from potion teachers. From what I've heard they're usually a lot more scattered, and garden oriented. I can't really picture Mrs. Housely as a get down in the dirt kind of a witch.

"Please take out your notebooks," she says before Ben steps into the classroom. "Mr. Light, you aren't part of this class."

"I'm sorry Mrs. Housely, but I have a message for Maddie. It's in regard to her training."

"Very well." She sweeps her arm in my direction, and Ben makes his way toward me. He's got one of his signature tiny smiles as his eye meets mine.

"Maddie." The boy greets me, stopping at my desk.

"Ben," I reply, raising my eyebrows as I wait for him to continue. We've never actually spoken before, so this is new.

"Aiden has been called away for the weekend, so no sessions today or tomorrow." He watches me for a moment, and I expect him to continue, but no. That's all I get. He nods, turning to go, and I surprise myself by reaching out. His arm is hot to the touch, and I drop it almost as fast as I grab it.

But my bravado is gone, and I can't find the words to ask him about Aiden. However, Ben surprises me once more. He steps close to my desk, his eyes intensely on mine.

"If you need anything, just yell."

It's such an odd thing to say, and that's when I realize all eyes are on us. I nod quickly, and Ben seems satisfied with my answer. He gives a parting wave to Mrs. Housley and then leaves. The rest of the class is looking at me, and instead of ducking my head, I meet their eye. The few close by avert their eyes, and I sit back a little satisfied with myself.

"What was that about?" Jade asks, as Mrs. Housely begins talking.

"I have no idea," I reply, opening up my notebook.

For the rest of the class, I take notes, but it's like I'm two different people. My mind is constantly drifting to Aiden. Where could he have gone? We're on lockdown and this is the second time he just disappeared. And what's the deal with sending Ben to tell me about it? He could've sent a note like last time. But no, he's being all weird about it. Which Ben was kind of weird about it too, and what is up with boys? Are they always this confusing, or did I just get a special batch?

❧ 23 ❧

All day I've been trying to figure out a way to sneak over to the library before the slumber party. Something has been bugging me, and I can't figure out if it may be a passage I read or a book I saw. It's like it's on the tip of my tongue, but I can't find the words to express myself. It's a frustrating feeling, on top of the frustration I feel at myself for caring about Aiden. Or the grumpiness I'm experiencing at the thought of the party. My emotions are definitely heightened, and I'm not sure I know what to do about it. Maybe I should see if I can go out to the pond again and release some of this magic brewing inside me.

"Are you ready for all the fun?" Jade asks as I walk into our room. She's sprawled out on her bed, a book in front of her, but she sits up as I head for my bed.

"Yes, I'm so excited," I say over my shoulder. My roommate doesn't reply, and I turn to see her watching me carefully.

"You don't want to do this?"

I sigh, because of course she can see that. I haven't been all that good at hiding my emotions lately. Must be because of the imbalance I'm feeling. I take a seat on my bed, facing my friend.

"Honestly, I'm not feeling up to anything right now. Also, I've never had a slumber party without my sisters, and I'm feeling a bit emotional about it."

"Is that all you're feeling emotional about?"

At that, I almost smile. Jade deserves much more credit than I've been giving her because she's been paying attention. I still haven't talked to her about my last encounter with Aiden, only because I don't even know what I would say. But maybe this is the opening I need.

"It's weird that Aiden has been gone," I begin, scooting backward to rest against the wall. "But maybe it's been for the best."

"How do you mean?"

"Last time we were together." I swallow audibly, fidgeting a little. "I almost kissed him."

"What?" Jade catapults off her bed and onto mine in one swift motion, which takes me completely by surprise. She tumbles into me and I laugh, trying to push her off.

"Jade!"

"Tell me everything!" She's not to be denied, so I rehash what that happened by the water. Jade listens completely enthralled, her arms wrapped around my pillow. When I'm finished speaking, Jade watches me for a long, quiet moment. Then, she pulls a Christy, squealing loudly and jumping in her seat.

"Oh, Maddie. I've been waiting for this to happen."

"Wait, what?"

"You've been circling each other for weeks. And all that tension and repressed... everything. I mean, ah!"

"Okay, slow your roll. It's not like we're getting together. It's me being all emotional and nearly ruining everything."

"Why would you ruin anything?" Jade seems genuinely confused, and I pause to collect my thoughts.

"It's not like he feels anything for me," I finally say. "And I have to keep training with him, which will make things super awkward. Plus, we're..." My words freeze before I can mention the library. "It would be weird. That's all."

Once again, Jade doesn't speak up right away, and when I glance over at her, she's got that contemplative look about her.

"What?"

"Nothing. You just seem to have made up your mind about the way he feels without actually talking to him."

I stare at my friend for a moment before I shake it off. There's absolutely no way I would tell Aiden what I've been thinking. That's just not something I'm ready to do. Or will ever be ready to do.

"No, thank you," is all I say, as I scoot off the bed. I head toward my dresser, pulling out my comfy and matching pajamas. Now, I'm even more unexcited about the girls coming over. I think hiding under the covers sounds like a much better use of my time.

"Okay, okay." Jade gives in, but I think that's only because she knows the girls are almost here, and I'm shutting down. It's not as if I'm ever really open with my feelings, and Jade knows not to push it.

What she said dances around in my mind as I change. I was planning on asking Jade her opinion after all, it doesn't matter if I don't like it. But she's right. I have already made up my mind about this because I know how things go. Yet, at the same time, people assuming anything about me is one of my greatest pet peeves. So, how do I talk to Aiden about this without revealing my feelings? Is there a way that conversation can be had without me showing all my cards?

"I don't think I'm brave enough to have that discussion," I say not turning around, but I know Jade can hear me. She stops doing whatever she's doing and waits for me to continue. After I pull my shirt over my head, I face her and she's watching me with support shining in her eyes.

"I can't even imagine being the first to share my feelings. I just can't," I say, shrugging.

"I get it, Maddie," Jade replies. "Honestly, I talk full of bravado, but I'm the same way. It's even scarier when it's someone you really care about."

"Is that where I am?" I ask honestly, because I have no idea about anything anymore. Most of all this.

"Only you can decide that for yourself," Jade replies, getting off the bed. "But while you do, we're going to watch a movie and eat a bunch of snacks and do our nails and not talk about it. And you're going to feel much better in the morning."

Reaching for my roommate, I give her a big hug and some of the tension seeps out of me as she returns it. Maybe having girl time won't be such a hassle after all. It'll be nice to keep my mind busy with something other than worries.

❦

THE GIRLS SHOW UP ABOUT TWENTY MINUTES LATER, ARMED with extra blankets and snacks. Christy is over-the-top hyper, which I'm used to. But even Vera seems to be enjoying herself as we make a pillow and blanket fort on the floor.

"Okay, so here is the list of activities." Christy pulls out a piece of paper as the rest of us exchange a look. This girl is really serious about her slumber partying. "Here are some snacks for consumption. We've got face masks and foot scrubs while we watch the first movie. Followed by manis and pedis, both or either, while we watch the second movie. Of course, it's important to hydrate, so there is plenty of water, and I was able to talk a certain lunch lady, who shall remain unnamed, into sneaking over some Coke as well."

Christy sweeps her hand over each item, the ultimate gameshow host, and I grin. This girl really does know how to party it up. Also, I haven't had soda in a very long time, so I don't even hesitate to reach for it.

"Ah, I knew that would be a winner! Let the festivities begin!"

The projector Christy was able to get is an old one, since the school doesn't really employ TV for education very often. Most of the teachers can conjure up whatever images we may need to see. But there are a few movies saved up for movie nights, and I grin as I look over at the selection.

"So, our options are a kid left behind at his house on Christmas, fighting aliens while looking for a way to protect earth from an oncoming evil, or sister witches?" I muse out loud. "That's quite some diversity."

"You really grabbed a witches movie for us to watch?" Vera comments, looking over my shoulder. Christy shrugs, already pulling out the face masks.

"I kind of really love their family." She goes back to unpacking all the essentials, some of which I've never even seen before. But then, I have one face wash that I'm loyal too and being a water witch, my complexion is fantastic.

"I vote for the alien movie," I say, and Vera nods.

"Me too!" Jade calls out as she heads to the bathroom. With the majority decided, we settle back as Christy explains the cleansing wipes she brought and the exfoliating brushes.

"This is intense," I mumble, receiving a very serious look from Christy.

"It's important to take care of your skin. That's how you become your own best friend."

I don't contradict the girl or comment any further. Clearly this is a big deal to her, and I'm never going to be the person that makes fun of other people's passions. That's one of the top lessons my parents taught me. It's amazing how I don't even think about these areas of life, but my family and my upbringing guides me in more ways than not.

My mind drifts back to the library and the nagging feeling I've had about it. Something jumped out at me last time I was there. I have to get back to those books tonight. Somehow.

We get our skin exfoliated and our masks on in the first thirty minutes of the movie. I've seen this one with my sisters, and it's always been a favorite. It doesn't help with the nostalgia I'm feeling, or how much I miss them, but that's okay. I'm learning, very slowly, how to own up to my own emotions. There's nothing wrong with what I'm feeling, I just need to use that to fuel me to move forward. And not get stuck in one spot.

As I glance around the room, I find that I'm truly enjoying myself, despite the sadness. These girls have become part of my school family, and I truly am lucky. It's so easy to concentrate on all the bad going on around me that I don't stop to appreciate the good. My dad has always taught me to remember the little details of life, and I've been missing out on that. Even though I didn't want the slumber party, I'm glad it happened.

"So, we should totally do a rating system," Christy announces much later. We've moved on to the witches movie and are working on our toe nails now.

"Rating for what?"

"The hotness in this school, of course!" Jade and I exchange a look at that, but Christy is already having too much fun. "I'll start. *Obvi* the shifters are on top of that list. I mean, Aiden? He's one hot alpha!" She giggles, and I grin. Even when he's not here, he's in everything I do.

"Vera, you go next!"

"I vote for Owen." The quiet girl surprises me. "I like the broody type." That actually makes sense.

"Oh, what about Mona?" Christy says, and I think back to the upperclassman Jade and I saw trying on a suit for the dance.

"That girl is gorgeous and fierce," Jade comments, and I nod.

"She's a shifter too," Vera says, and we burst out laughing.

"Of course they're all shifters," I say, when we've settled a little. "Vera, you're on that list too. There's something about shifters. The pack in my hometown? They're all beautiful creatures."

Vera blushes, but doesn't comment. I realize I put her on the spot, but I can clearly see she's pleased.

"I wouldn't mind me a shifter," Christy comments, wiggling her eyebrows up and down, and we're laughing once again.

When our nails are painted, and the whole place smells like Autumn morning at home, I snuggle down into my side of the blanket fort, eyes glued to the screen. We talked, we laughed, and it finally felt like I was just a girl, hanging out with friends. Now, I just need to wait for them to fall asleep, so I can get down to the library. No matter how relaxed I am, I won't be able to sleep until I figure out what's been bugging me.

❧ 24 ❧

"Should you be sneaking around out here?"

I'm very proud of myself for not jumping at the quiet voice, but truth be told, I was expecting this. Just a little. Turning slowly, I narrow my eyes as a figure steps from the shadows.

"Ben, are you a creepy stalker?"

"Well, not creepy." He flashes me a grin, and I fight the urge to return it. I had a feeling I'd be seeing more of him while Aiden is away, so there's another pat on the back for me.

"Shouldn't you be on the opposite side of the castle, I don't know, sleeping?"

"I could be asking you the same thing." Ben takes a step closer. "Aren't you in the midst of an all-girl slumber party?"

"How do you—" I stop as he grins at me again. This shifter has no problem wearing his smile for all to see, and I have to fight the urge to return it. But if I don't get a move on, I'll either get caught or... actually, just get caught.

That's bad enough.

"Well, I'll be going now," I say, waving a hand in his general direction. But after I've taken barely three steps, Ben is beside me. "Can I help you with something?"

"Sure. You can pretend you won't argue with me when I tell you I'm to escort you to wherever you're going."

"I can pretend, but not for long." I snort, very un-lady like. Ben chuckles at the sound and despite how weird this situation is to me, I can feel a comradeship forming between us.

"Why are you here, Ben?" I decide to not beat around the bush. Ben gives me a long look, as if contemplating whether or not he'll tell me the truth.

"Aiden asked me."

For some reason, I'm not surprised. But Ben's words still bring a pang to my chest, and a sense of awareness I try so hard to suppress.

It's difficult to ignore my feelings when Aiden keeps doing these little things. In his own way, he keeps taking care of me, and I'm not particularly sure what to do with that.

"There's absolutely no chance in you letting me be?" I ask, looking Ben in the eye. He shakes his head in response, and I don't waste another minute. We need to move before the patrol comes by. It was hard enough sneaking away from the girls. The charms of protection I made last time are still in my pocket, but I didn't have time to replenish the magic. A part of me was nervous that if I did, the headmaster would notice. I have to use what I can and can't waste any opportunities I get.

I rush down the hall, Ben close on my heels. He stays true to his word and doesn't question where we're going. But I can tell he wants to. I mean, who wouldn't?

Suddenly, he grabs my hand, pulling me behind one of the columns. I'm smart enough not to make a sound as we squeeze in between the wall and the marble. A few moments later, one of the patrol guys rounds the corner. My vision isn't as great as a shifter's, but I can see him glance down the hall, before moving on. Ben puts a finger to his lips, and I nod. We have to wait for him to get farther away.

When Ben deems it safe again, he steps out into the hall,

pulling me with him. He does another quick study before motioning me to move.

"Thanks," I say, and he smiles in return. It really is nifty having a shifter around. We continue creeping down the hall before we arrive at the back staircase. This is riskier, but it'll put us right near the greenhouse.

"Can you go first?"

Ben takes the lead without question, and I follow closely behind. I'm still not sure what I'm going to do with him when we get to the greenhouse. It's not as if I want more people to know about the library. I'm constantly contemplating what to do with the knowledge and how it's protecting itself. Maybe I should trust that the spell wouldn't allow anyone who's a danger to the place to know about it. It had no problem with Kate or Liam or even Aiden. So, I can't say I tested out that theory fully. I have a feeling the library won't have a problem with Ben either.

We reach the greenhouse with no problems, and I know it's only because of Ben. The security has been heightened, and I might not have made it this far alone.

"What now?" Ben asks once we're inside, and I stand looking around at the plants.

"Now you leave?" I reply, hopefully.

"No chance of that. I'm not about to go against my alpha's orders."

Of course not. I mull over my next move, but I really just have the one. Ben is about to find out about my secret.

"Okay, I assume since your alpha told you to protect me that means in all areas of my life?" Ben gives me a puzzling look as I continue. "What I'm about to show you is a secret. A secret that only four people know about, and it has to stay that way."

"Maddie, don't worry. Your secret is safe with me."

The way he says it, and the way he looks at me, I believe it. Having no other choice left, I head toward the corner of the greenhouse and unmask my little hideaway door. Ben stays quiet throughout the whole process, but I can read the surprise in his eyes. He definitely didn't expect this. Which means Aiden didn't prepare him and has kept my secret. I'm thankful for that because I'm almost positive, even with protective charms, an alpha would have a way around witch's magic if it came down to it.

When we reach the door to the library, I place my hand against it, and it glows i's welcoming light. Once inside, Ben is just as enamored with the place as I've been, but he still doesn't ask any questions. Deciding I'm stuck with him, I give him a quick summary of the place.

"This is incredible, Maddie. And no one knows?"

"I can't even talk about it outside of here. One day I'll figure out what that means, but right now I need to find the book I was looking at last time. Something has been bothering me for days."

Leaving Ben to explore on his own, I head toward the table Aiden and I sat at last time. My mind brings up an image of us there, but I push it away. I really have no business thinking about a boy right now.

Picking up book after book I try to pinpoint the feeling I've been carrying around. If it was something I read, I'd have to go through every page. But if it was something else, maybe I can rely on my intuition. Ben has moved closer and is watching me now but doesn't speak. I appreciate that, and I realize I kind of like having him around. He reminds me of Liam a bit. I find his presence sort of comforting.

"It's not working!" I finally snap, dropping the last book on the table.

"What is it you're looking for?"

"I'm not sure and that's the problem. The last time," I take a deep breath, "it was as if something reached out to me through the pages. And now I can't find that feeling."

"Maybe you're here with the wrong guy."

My eyes fly up to meet his, and I see him shrug.

"It's not like that," I hurry on to say.

"I just mean you and Aiden have a certain... magic about you.

You're a Hawthorne. He's the next alpha. Maybe that's the energy that's needed."

It does make sense, but I also think Ben is talking about something else. I try not to read too much into it, but the magic aspect does give me an idea.

"Let me try something."

I spread out the books on the table in front of me, before climbing on a chair. Standing over the array of hardcovers, I close my eyes and hover my arms over the table. There isn't a specific spell I can try, but maybe I can just ask for the answer. I've seen Bri do this once or twice but have never tried it myself.

The magic inside of me begins to tingle, spreading slowly at first, then building faster and faster. My whole body feels like it's on fire as I push the magic to do my bidding. I ask it nicely, to show me what I'm searching for, keeping my intention as pure as possible.

"Maddie." After what seems like hours, Ben calls my name softly. I open my eyes and glance down to see one book glowing just slightly.

A grin blossoms onto my face as I reign my magic in and jump down.

"Okay, let's see what all the fuss is about."

۞

IT'S ANOTHER HOUR BEFORE I FINALLY FIND SOMETHING.

Ben has been sitting quietly, browsing through one of the books. But the moment my eye lands on the right page, it's like he can sense it. I feel him move closer, yet I don't take my eyes off the page.

It's a list of families, witch families, going back hundreds and hundreds of years. The page unfolds, a tree growing right there on paper. So many names, so much history.

"What is it?" I didn't realize he moved to the table and is now sitting beside me.

"It's a family tree. Of magic. These names go back hundreds of years."

"On this one spread of paper?"

"It's magic," I reply, smiling. I see the names change and move as I go further and further back.

"This is what you were looking for?"

"Yes. I didn't see the actual tree last time, but this page," I turn two pages back, "it speaks of a dark history of witches, and that's what has been on my mind."

"What do you mean?"

"My dad is a Watcher," I begin, turning my attention to the boy in front of me. "He's been a keeper of magical knowledge his whole life, and he's shared a lot of it with me. Not everything, obviously. I didn't know the Ancients were anything but a bedtime story until they started rising right outside of my home town."

"But isn't that the case with everyone? Even my pack assumed the Ancients weren't real."

"It's part of their plan. To be so forgotten that we're not ready to defend ourselves. But they've made waves in our lives before."

"When?"

"Well, I can tell you that thirty-five years ago, in Hawthorne, they sent a plague that nearly wiped out the town."

"I didn't know that."

"I didn't either. But my parents did. They were both there." He's silent for a bit as I continue to study the names.

"How does that help you now?"

"It helps because every family keeps a grimoire. It holds their individual spells, history of their time, charms that pertain only to them. If I can find some of the older families maybe they have information on the Ancients. The further back we go, the more chance we have of finding something new we can use. If my parents had dealings with the Ancients thirty-five years ago, can you imagine someone from three hundred years ago?"

"But wouldn't that information be readily available?"

"You'd think so, but no. Remember the Salem witch trials? Just one of the many times humans made it difficult for us to be part of the world. Families kept their secret and their grimoires under lock and key. There are so many covens out there that we have no idea about. This may be what helps us uncover those secrets."

I grab one of the notebooks I left here last semester and a pen and begin jotting down the names as they come up on the page. Ben lets me be, and we stay like that for a while. My mind races with possibilities and everything we can learn from this. I'll have to find a way to get the information to my sisters since they'll have a much better chance at figuring this out.

When I think I've copied down enough names, I take a piece of paper and bookmark the page. Then I stand.

"Ready to get back?" Ben asks, also standing. I nod, folding the paper and tucking it into my jeans. With one last look at the library, I lead the way out.

Once we're back in the greenhouse, a sense of dread reaches out to me. I can't pinpoint the feeling, but it's there, and I turn to Ben automatically.

"Do you feel—"

But I never get to finish. The whole school begins to shake, the ground unsteady under my feet.

"Ben?"

He grabs my hand, pulling me away from the falling shelves and into the hallway. I'm having a difficult time staying upright as the school trembles a few more times.

"What's happening?"

"Come on. We need to get out of here." Ben pulls me behind him as one of the pictures hanging on the wall shatters at our backs. The case displaying various potions topples over, making us jump back. The alarm begins to sound, shrieking commands at us.

"Can we get outside?" I yell over the noise and Ben shakes his head. The whole school is on its nightly lock down. I focus on the alarm long enough to hear the instructions. We need to be in a room, protected. And we're not.

"Where is the patrol?" I ask, thinking of the other people who would be out of their protective rooms.

"There are designated rooms for them," Ben shouts back, because of course there are. They wouldn't let students patrol if there wasn't a backup plan. The school shudders again, this one stronger than the last, knocking us off our feet. I land hard, on all fours, my palms and knees stinging from the impact.

"Come on." Ben reaches for me, picking me up and setting me on my feet, before we take off deeper into the school. Having no other choice, I rush after him as the school continues to shake around us. Glass shatters and the next thing I know, Ben is wrapping himself around me, tucking my face into his chest.

"You okay?" he asks, glancing down, and I manage a nod. This is definitely not how I imagined my night going. Ben grabs my hand once more, and we're moving. Another minute and he stops abruptly in front of a door.

Yanking it open, he pulls us in, shutting it behind. I stumble over my own feet and whatever is in the room, but even in near darkness, Ben manages to catch me.

"Can you work some light magic?" he asks and I nod, even though he probably can't see me. Illumination spell is one of the first ones I learned as a kid. Two waves of a hand and a few words, "Light the way, please."

An orb appears in my hand, and I glance around to find us in a storage closet. I look at the shelves full of items, but nothing is moving.

"How are we protected?"

"I'm thinking, even though it's a closet, it's still a room. The protective spell is in place." He shrugs, but he's a smart one, that's for sure.

We each take a seat on the floor, exhausted from the night. My mind keeps wandering back to what's going on outside this room, but we won't be going out there any time soon.

"What do you think is happening to the school?" Ben finally asks. I don't answer right away, trying to push away the panic.

"I think someone is doing their best to destroy it."

25

"Thank you for getting me out of there," I say, breaking the silence. We've been trying to listen to the sounds of the school, but it's as if we've been sealed inside of a cocoon. Every now and then a noise will reach us, but it sounds too far away to distinguish it.

"Anytime," Ben replies, sliding around to get more comfortable. We're sitting with our backs against the storage shelf, my legs criss-crossed in front of me, his pulled up at the knees. "What do you think is going on out there?"

"I think the faculty is doing a sweep, making sure no one penetrated the school's grounds," I reply automatically. "It's standard protocol. If someone did get in, I think we would've heard something by now."

Ben nods but doesn't comment and we fall back into silence. My mind is working overtime. These breeches are getting more frequent. Every single time the alarm goes off, I'm scared it will be it. That the evil will invade and this place will fall down around us. I can't imagine Thunderbird Academy not standing tall, but it's such a possibility now, it makes my chest hurt.

"Can I ask you about what happened in Hawthorne?"

A part of me expected this. It's a question everyone has been wanting to ask since the moment I returned. But besides my close friend group, no one else has approached me.

"It's okay if you don't want to talk about it," Ben hurries on to add, but I wave it off.

"There's not much to tell," I begin, resigned to talking about it. I do kind of owe Ben for tonight. This is the least I can do. "I found some information. Much like I found it today." Once again, I can't quite mention the library, and it's a bit annoying. "My sisters already had all the pieces. They just needed the missing part. I think they would've figured it out without me. It just would've taken them longer."

"And might've cost them more." I glance up at him at his words. "I don't think you should minimize your part in this."

"It's not like I'm trying to." I sigh, wondering how much to tell him. For some reason, I feel comfortable with him. And I'm not sure if it's because he's Aiden's friend or because I'm being a little more open to relationships now. But maybe it's simply because I don't know him, and I need to talk to someone.

"It's just that people expect more from me because I was part of this great spell. But truth be told, I didn't even do much. My magic may have grown recently, but I'm still nowhere near where people expect me to be."

"That's understandable. But Maddie." He leans forward, intensity written all over his face. "Aiden has told me just how skillful you are. You're smart and powerful. Selling yourself short won't help anyone. Most of all you."

He leans back as if he hasn't just delivered one of the most amazing encouragements. Of course, he wouldn't know how much those words mean to me, or how I'm soaking them up like a flower who hasn't been watered in a while.

The interesting part is that it's not as if I need a confidence boost, per se. I know my own power. I know there is a lot I can handle. I'm growing stronger with every test sent my way, every challenge. I'm not the same girl I was when I started here a year ago. Sometimes I forget that year even existed. Everything is so different now. But the doubts reach even the most confident of individuals and having Aiden's faith in me so blatantly spoken of makes me feel all warm and fuzzy inside.

Everyone can use a little of faith in them now and then. Apparently, I have that support in Aiden. Even though he won't tell me so himself.

"Thanks, Ben," I finally say, just as the door clicks before being pulled open.

"Madison Hawthorne. Why am I not even surprised?" Headmaster Marković asks, stepping into the doorway, the light at his back.

I stand, shrugging.

"I'm just lucky, I guess."

"WOULD YOU LIKE TO EXPLAIN TO ME WHAT YOU WERE DOING, hiding in the storage room?" Headmaster Marković asks me a little later, as I sit in his office. The school is awake, students being interviewed as the faculty continues to comb through the grounds.

"It was the first place that was available after the alarm went off?" I reply, receiving a very unamused look from the headmaster.

"Maddie."

"I couldn't sleep," I say, going back to my prepared excuse. "My magic was a little restless, and I needed it calmed before it went haywire."

"So, you went to..."

"The greenhouse. The plants there helped."

Even though I know he's still suspicious, he can't deny the logic. As an elemental witch, the best place I can be is near nature. Since I can't go outside at night, the greenhouse would be the most plausible solution.

"How did Mr. Light end up in the same place as you?"

"We ran into each other when he was on patrol." I really hope he's actually scheduled to patrol and wasn't out of his room just because of me. I guess right because headmaster doesn't question me further.

"Where is he?" I ask, still afraid I got the shifter in trouble.

"He's been called away by his alpha."

My heart jumps in my chest, a dozen questions on the tip of my tongue. But I doubt Headmaster is in a sharing mood, so I don't ask.

"Am I free to go?" I ask instead and receive a go ahead. When I leave the headmaster's office, I'm met by groups of students huddled in the hallways wearing their pajamas. Miss Cindy is handing out cups of tea, trying to soothe them as best as she can. Without meeting anyone's eye, I hurry to my side of the castle, my mind on the shifter. For Ben to be pulled away, something had to have happened.

"Oh my word, Maddie!" Jade throws her arms around me the moment I reach our room. The girls are sitting with blankets wrapped around them on the floor, a worried look on their faces. "Where have you been?"

"In the headmaster's office," I reply, returning her hug. I don't really want to get into it with Vera and Christy here, and I give Jade an extra squeeze to keep her quiet. She seems to read my mind and doesn't press.

"What is going on, Maddie?" Christy asks, her eyes big and round.

"I'm not sure. They didn't say anything, but they're interviewing a bunch of people."

"They did come by and check on us, but we were all sleeping when the alert sounded. So, we didn't have anything to add," Jade explains as I settle back on my bed.

Exhausted from the events of tonight, I lay down, still fully dressed, as the girls continue talking. My body goes numb, but my mind won't stop working. So many possibilities rush through, none of them with good outcomes. It scares me to think that someone in this school wishes it harm.

Mentally, I try to put together a list of suspects, but I have no idea where to start. It's not like there are any stereotypical signs I can follow. With magic, anything is possible. The sweetest person can be the darkest witch. I could never put anyone into a box. It's with these thoughts that I let myself drift off into sleep.

THE NEXT MORNING, THE WHOLE SCHOOL IS IN UPROAR. THERE'S a shadow hanging over the school, a heaviness that's finally descended upon us. When I woke up this morning, clouds made everything look gloomy.

"This weather is weird, right?" Jade asks on the way to our second class. The first hour was skipped and replaced with an assembly, but Headmaster Marković had nothing new to add. The school is still on lockdown. Magic is still being monitored closely. We can't wander off. This place no longer feels like a sanctuary. It's more of a prison.

"Typically, the weather is regulated by the upperclassmen elementals," I reply, my eyes scanning over every person we pass. I told myself I'd be more on alert, but it's hard. These are my fellow classmates. I can't get over the fact that one of them may be a traitor.

"So, why isn't it?"

"Maybe it is," I shrug, glancing at my friend. "We need gloomy days to balance the sunny ones, right?"

Jade takes that at face value, but I know she's not reassured. I'm not either. Something is happening, and the weather is just one aspect of that. It's not like the elementals watch it continuously, but they do help out when it gets too bad. It looks like an apocalypse is coming, so I would assume they'd do something. Unless they can't.

The rest of the day isn't much better. There are whispers and looks, and no one is trusting anyone. Aiden is still gone, and Ben has followed him apparently. I wonder what could be so important that the academy would break their rules and let them out.

"You doing okay?" Noel asks, coming up to stand beside me. I've been nestled between the wall and the bookcase, watching students rush by. I'm in observation mode, trying to piece together all the clues that have been showing up. At least, I think there are clues. Watching people's behaviors is a little exhausting, but necessary. I haven't been paying as much attention as I should've been. But I'm paying attention now.

"Sure. How about you?"

"Honestly, a little freaked out. They almost got in." That gets my attention. I turn fully to Noel.

"What?"

"I overheard one of the upperclassmen talking. The attack almost pierced through the protective shield. They almost got in."

That's news to me, but I'm not that surprised. It was going to happen eventually. There is a sense of foreboding that we've been living with, waiting for that other shoe to drop. The Ancients will never give up, and this school is of interest to them. Maybe this is happening with every academy. Maybe the plan here is to infiltrate the young minds. If I was masterminding a world domination, that's where I would start.

"What else did you hear?" I lean my shoulder against the wall so I can watch Noel and the crowd in front of us.

"The headmaster is putting together a plan of action. I'm not sure what he's thinking he can do at this point that they haven't already been doing, but it's something. That's all I know."

"It does make sense. They have to try everything. Especially since whatever they are doing is not working."

We fall silent as another few students rush by us, two of the girls giving me a quick once-over.

"Does that get tiring?" Noel nods toward the girls.

"You have no idea."

I push away from the wall, and Noel follows close beside me. We're heading away from the lunchroom, and I know I told the girls I'd meet them there, but I have no desire to be subjected to that many people at the same time.

"I'm going to head outside," I tell Noel, and at first, he seems like he's going to stop me. Instead, he gives me a long searching look, before inclining his head.

"Be careful, okay?"

"You too."

I leave him behind, and when I'm at the end of the hallway, I turn to see him disappearing into the crowd. With everything that's been going on, I haven't really taken the time to appreciate my friends lately. But I have been given some pretty good ones, and I make a mental note to focus on that a little more. If we survive this.

When the fresh air hits my cheeks, I breathe in fully. There are students and faculty on the stairs in front of the school building as well, but I walk past them without a second look. The paper with names is still burning a hole in my pants, and I need to find a way to relay the information to my sisters. I would go to the headmaster, but I'm not sure if there is a way to explain to him where I got the information without breaking the library's rules. I still have to figure out how to get around that.

I head straight down to the avenue of limes without any definite destination in mind. What I wouldn't give to speak to my dad right now. He would be able to make sense of all of this. I just know it. Even his presence is calming, and he has that air of knowledge about him that I've always found endearing. But these thoughts don't bring comfort, only pain. Even after months, I still have no idea how to find him, and there are no clues left to follow. I wanted to come back to Thunderbird Academy so I could help search for him the best way he taught me, and I've done absolutely nothing to reach that goal.

Not only am I failing as a friend, I have failed as a daughter.

Today is apparently a day for a pity party. If I was going to be mature about the situation, I could tell myself that it's not my fault. That I'm not responsible for what happened to him. But I feel the weight of his absence on me like a heaviness I cannot shake off. It's like everything around me is falling apart, and I am completely helpless.

But I'm not helpless. I can't let myself fall so far down this hole that I never claw my way out. My dad would say I have to pang-wangle, and he would be correct. In spite of everything that's going on, I have no choice but to fight.

This school is no longer the safe haven I so desperately searched for, and I can't sit by and do nothing about it. Just like that, the pity party is over. I'm pulling myself together, even if that's only because it's the one thing I have left to do. If everyone is going to think I'm this great witch, I better start acting like it.

❧ 26 ❧

It's been close to a week and everything has been quiet. I've spent as much time as I can at the library, but I've found nothing helpful about the attacks. I have been able to find a few protective spells I can try, and I've been working on memorizing and practicing them. At this point, I may need to use them sooner than I anticipate.

The only other piece of information I could decipher are the ancient trials. Apparently, the Ancients held competitions with each other, trying to one up each other in various ways. If they're targeting schools now, maybe it's about the number. Or the individuals who go there. It's not exactly helpful, but at least it provides more of a motive for recruitment and these attacks.

This morning I felt unsettled, and when I step into the dining room, the feeling doesn't go away. It intensifies. It's as if my whole body has just broken out in goosebumps, but I can't pinpoint the source.

"What's up?" Noel asks, sensing my hesitation.

"I'm not sure. It's like there's a disturbance in the force." His smile is quick at my reference, but I'm not trying to be funny. Something is coming, but I don't know what. I scan the room but find nothing out of sorts. My friends move through the line, and I follow them automatically.

It seems that everyone is taking lunch at the same time today because the place is full. All the tables are taken, so we resign ourselves to going outside.

"Are we sure? It's kind of chilly out there," Christy whines, but follows us anyway. Truth be told, I'm happy to be out here. I needed to get out of that room. Not sure I could eat in there when I'm feeling so unbalanced.

The air has turned cool in the last week, as if Autumn finally decided to make her appearance. This time of the year is Bri's favorite, and I wonder if she had time to plant her herbs with all the craziness that's been going on.

"Oh, come on, Christy," I hear Jade say, "It'll be freezing before we know it, and then we'll wish we were out here."

I have to agree with my friend on that one. Even though the upperclassmen weather witches regulate much of the seasons here, they stay true to the rest of the world. After all, there is a reason why everything goes through seasons. Kind of like we do. Being at Thunderbird Academy is a season now. We find one of the unoccupied tables outside, taking a seat. The air is refreshing on my flushed skin, and I close my eyes for a second to enjoy the gentle breeze.

"Umm, Maddie." Jade's voice breaks through my moment of peace, and I turn to find her smiling at me. "Why don't we go get more juice?"

I glance down at the two bottles in front of us, confused by Jade's sudden behavior. She's still smiling at me, but I can tell it's a little strained.

"I think I'm good, thanks."

"You sure you don't want anything else?" This comes from Noel, who's sitting on my other side. I glance between my two friends, wondering what has gotten into them, when a shadow falls across my plate. I turn to look up and find Ben grinning down at me.

"Hey, Maddie!"

"Ben, you're back." I point out the obvious, as the boy rocks back on his heels. "Everything okay?"

"Somewhat." He shrugs.

"Maddie." Jade calls my name again as she places her hand on my arm. "I think we should go get some fruit."

"Jade, I'm fine, really. Ben," I say to the boy behind me. "Would you like..."

The question dies on my lips as he drifts to the side, opening up my view past his back. There's a group right by the doors we walked out of earlier. I recognize all the faces but one.

A gorgeous, dark-haired girl has her arms around Aiden's waist, gazing up at him like he's the love of her life. His eyes are on me.

I feel that look inside me, igniting and destroying parts of me all at once. The intensity steals my breath and shatters my thoughts, and I can't look away no matter how much I want to.

Ben steps back in front of me cutting off my view, and a gust of air rushes into my lungs.

"Maddie?"

"I guess Aiden is back too," I manage, knowing full well the shifter can hear everything we're saying.

"Who's the girl?" Christy asks, and I turn around to find my friends' eyes on me. Jade and Noel's behavior is understandable now. They were trying to protect me. Christy isn't paying attention to me though, she's looking over my shoulder.

"That's Natalie. She's Aiden's... betrothed."

For a moment, I don't think I heard Ben right. The wood on the table becomes crystal clear, as if all my senses are now completely focused on the spot in front of me. I feel a movement at my back, and then Ben takes a seat on the other side of Noel. Christy laughs, but the sound is hollow and far away.

"Betrothed? Is that a thing?"

"It is in our world." Ben shrugs, grabbing a piece of bread off my plate. I can feel his eyes on me, but I'm too stunned to organize my thoughts. I still can't seem to raise my head or articulate any of the words forming in my mind.

"How so?" I hear Vera ask softly. Or maybe I just can't hear well over the hum in my ears.

"Nat is going to be the Alpha of her pack. Aiden is the Alpha of his. It's a business arrangement."

"That's a little..." Jade begins but stops herself.

"Dated?" Ben finishes for her, and I can almost hear the shrug in his voice. "It's all we know. Oh hey, guys."

I'm trying really hard to find my footing, but even though I'm sitting down, I feel like the whole world is tilting under my feet. It's like I'm back inside the school during the earthquake. The group has moved toward us, and I can still feel Aiden's eyes on me, burning a mark into my back. Noel scoots just a tad closer, placing his hand on mine under the table, and I barely feel it. Then, a soft growl reaches my ears and that one sound is what finally snaps me back to reality.

Raising my head, I turn, meeting Aiden's eyes. I don't have to look to know that growl came from him because he doesn't miss Noel's move to comfort me.

"Everyone meet Natalie," Ben says while Aiden and I continue our stare down. I think I'm moving past shocked and straight into sad, so I need to escape somewhere before I make a scene.

"Welcome to Thunderbird Academy," Christy pipes up, grinning.

"Yeah, thanks." Natalie's voice is just as gorgeous as she is. When I finally look at her, I realize that she's the kind of girl countries go to war over. Smooth, tanned skin, large brown eyes, and lips as plump and red as a cherry. Everyone introduces themselves and when it's my turn, I'm not sure what to do.

My heart crumbles like a piece of paper in a clutched hand. Suddenly, I can't breathe and everything in me wants to flee, but I stay put. And I put on a smile.

"I'm Maddie," I find myself saying, "It's nice to meet you, Natalie."

❧

THE TABLE STAYS SILENT AS I FINISH MY INTRODUCTION, AND
the girl in front of me gives me a quick study before turning to
Aiden.

"We should really get going. Not to be rude," she hurries to
add. Her smile is full and blinding, and I think I'm going to burst
into tears any minute.

"I'll see you later," I hear Ben say, and I force myself to look at
him and nod. Apparently, our little adventure has bonded us, and
I'm glad. I like the guy. But right now, I want to hide from every
shifter I know and never allow myself to feel anything ever again.

They move away without a word, and I realize the others didn't
even speak up. Owen has always been silent and watchful, and I
wonder how much he truly sees. There's a moment of silence as
we're left on our own.

"Gosh, she's gorgeous," Christy breaths out, and I lose it.
Standing quickly, I push past Noel and Jade, racing into the opposite direction the group went. I hear my name called, but I can't be
there right now. Blindly, I run toward the pond, the need to scream
almost overwhelming me.

I let myself be in this situation. I allowed myself to develop
feelings for a guy who was never going to be mine, and now that
he's not, I'm broken inside. And I don't know how to put myself
together.

With the whole world falling apart around me, what a stupid
thing it is to fall for a guy.

When I reach the pond, I'm out of breath. But it doesn't stop
the magic building up inside me. I stumble right into the dirt at
the bank and then I let it all out. The scream rips out of me as I
thrust my arms into the water. The magic ignites, blinding me for a
second, before the whole pond lifts up, hovering in the sky. The
anger at myself, the sadness at the situation, the frustration, all
pour out through my body as it shakes with power. The water
begins to disperse, flying with the speed of a bullet in different

directions. A second before it becomes too late, I realize what I'm doing, and I pull it all back.

The water snaps back into the pond, splashing over the side. A wave comes over me, soaking me to the core, but I don't care to protect myself from it. I fall onto my back, looking up at the sky while I force myself to breath normally. My body feels numb, as if I've just spent hours training, but somehow, exhilarated at the same time.

Slowly, I sit up, glancing at the water now resting calmly in its original space. How can I be so dumb as to fall for a guy I knew could never like me the same way? My sisters' fairytale love stories have blinded me to reality. Not that I would ever fault them for that. I love that they found happiness. I just hope one day I can have someone look at me the way Connor looks at Harper or Mark looks at Bri. Like they're their whole world and nothing can tear them apart.

I give myself another few moments as my magic completely calms inside of me. That was quite the outburst, and since the school is under even more monitoring than usual, I probably set off some alarms. Which means I really need to go tell the headmaster I'm the one causing the waves and not the Ancients.

Pulling the water out of my clothes, I'm dry once more. I square my shoulders and put on a brave face. I can't allow anyone to see just how much this situation is bothering me. Jade and Noel already know because I'm a lot more transparent around them. But I don't need Ben to know. I definitely don't need Aiden to figure it out.

When I'm back inside the building, I head straight to the headmaster's office. The hallways are still full of students, even though most of the classes are finished for the day. No one wants to separate themselves from the herd. There is strength in numbers, after all. Miss Cindy doesn't hesitate to buzz me in, as if she's been waiting for me. Which I wouldn't be surprised if she was. She's an elemental witch as well, and she's connected to the school. I'm sure she felt my magic release just like headmaster did.

"Miss Hawthorne." He greets me as I step into his office. "How lovely to see you again."

"I'm sorry," I blurt out, stopping right in front of his desk. "I didn't mean to set off any alarms. I just really needed to let it go, my magic has been building and it's been difficult..."

"Miss Hawthorne," he interrupts motioning to the chair. "Please take a seat."

I sit immediately, worried and confused. I didn't exactly expect him to be so calm about the whole thing. I know how on edge everyone has been, especially the staff. It's not easy to be responsible for so many students and their safety.

"You're not mad?" I finally ask, when Headmaster doesn't automatically get into it.

"To tell you the truth, I am surprised it has taken you this long to practice your magic to this extent."

"What?"

"Miss Hawthorne, we both know you come from a very powerful family and are a powerful witch yourself." Headmaster Marković leans forward, linking his fingers in front of him. "The need to allow your magic to run free will grow, just as your powers will. We have been monitoring your magical signature since the day you returned to school. And every time we have met since then, I have watched and encouraged you. Maybe not as well as I hoped."

"Oh." Well, that answers a lot of the questions I had. This is how they're watching for traitors too, I'm almost positive. But this means they also know when I'm in the library.

"You've watched me this *whole* time?" I ask, putting emphasis on the word. Headmaster Marković gives me one of his rare smiles, before replying.

"Yes. But your magic is not always discernible. Care to tell me about it?"

"I would," I reply honestly. "But I also can't. I found something that may be of help, but it seems to have a protection spell over it, which causes me to keep it a secret." Even those words are difficult to utter, but Headmaster doesn't seem surprised.

"There are places within these grounds that are unknown even to me. Magic has a way of choosing us, and when it does, we do not ask questions. We follow where it leads. If this... whatever it may be... has chosen you, you are accountable to it, and I hope you use it wisely."

His words calm my fears and make me braver at the same time. If he believes in me enough to let me have this secret, I can't let him down. I can't let the school down. Which is what inspires my next words.

"I need you to send my sisters a bit of information, and I need permission to be out of my room after dark."

27

The next few days, I do my best to avoid Aiden. And the rest of his pack. It's not as easy as it sounds considering our paths cross a lot more throughout the day than I originally anticipated. It's like they're everywhere. After receiving special permission from the headmaster to be out of my room at night, I've been spending a lot of time at the library. My sisters haven't gotten back to me about the ancestry, but they did praise my thinking. Bri mentioned there have been times when a witch can call on her ancestors at a time of need. It's a practiced skill, and an old one that hasn't been used for generations. But they're doing their research while I continue mine.

The more I learn about the Ancients, the more worried I become. There's no way of tracking them, no way to predict their next move. If they were truly the ones who took my dad, I have no way of finding them.

At least I get a little break when I'm in my witch classes. No shifters here, unless they share witch's blood. And there are only a few in the school like that. None of them is Natalie.

"Maddie, wait up!" My luck runs out when I step out of my potions class and hear Ben calling my name. I turn to watch him jog up to me, a grin on his face. Since I'm not actually mad at him, I can't keep myself from responding.

"What's up?"

"I just wanted to make sure you knew there was training today." He looks very uncomfortable delivering the news, and I can't blame him. Aiden has deemed him the one to make these announcements to me, and Ben would have to be blind not to see how unsettling it has become between his alpha and me.

"Sure. I thought so." I try on a smile, before turning to go. I have no intention of going, but I figured someone would tell me eventually.

"I'm sorry." Ben's words stop me, and I glance over my shoulder. Jade moves away with the girls, leaving Ben and I by ourselves.

"What do you have to be sorry about?"

"Making this awkward for you." he rubs the back of his neck, stealing small glances at me, as if he's not sure of his reception. And I guess maybe this is awkward for him. We're new friends, and he's been put into a situation where he's literally the bearer of bad news.

"Hey," I begin, placing a hand on his arm to stop his fidgeting. For big-bad-wolves, these boys really are just teenagers. I forget that sometimes. We're not that different after all. "You and me? We're solid. That's not going to change."

He gives me a blinding smile, and I answer in kind. But just as quickly as it comes, it dies away when I hear a growl behind me. Ben hastily takes a step away, his eyes over my shoulder, and I don't need to turn to know who's behind me.

"Ben." I address the guy once more and his eyes drop down to mine. "I'll see you later, okay?" Then, without another word, I pivot and leave them behind. I can't make myself look at Aiden, and so I don't. Technically, it's not his fault I had feelings he didn't reciprocate. But then again, I thought he did. And that makes me angry at myself. Angry enough not to be around him.

"Are you going to keep ignoring me?" Aiden's voice reaches me as I step outside the school's front doors. I've been spending a lot of time outside lately, when I'm not in the library. Not that Aiden needs to know my routine to find me. He's never had any trouble with that.

"I'm not ignoring you," I reply, moving down the stairs. "I'm busy."

"Busy ignoring me." It's a statement not a question, so I don't bother replying. Of course, he follows me down the steps and onto the pathway.

"What do you want?" I finally break the silence stopping to face him, because I know he'll just follow me around if I don't.

"You haven't come to training." He's right. I've avoided training for two days now and was about to do it again.

"And you've come to fetch me yourself? I thought you had people for that." I don't even bother to mask my annoyance as I glare at Aiden. He's not deterred though. I don't think I'll ever see him unsettled. At least, not in the way he makes me every time he's around.

"I won't apologize for telling Ben to keep an eye on you, Duchess."

"No, of course not. But it's okay. Ben and I are... friends now." I smile big as Aiden's eyes flash. Maybe I do get under his skin a little. "But I don't need a babysitter," I finish, folding my arms in front of me.

"That wasn't—"

"Don't you have your girlfriend to take care of?" I interrupt and watch his eyes narrow, but I'm not backing down.

"Maddie..." He starts again after a small pause, but I can't deal with him anymore. I especially can't deal with him when he uses my name like that.

"I need a break." I cut him off once more. There is absolutely no desire in me to know more about Natalie or his responsibility to her.

He watches me for a long moment, and it's hard not to fidget under that gaze. I feel like he sees right into me. But I keep my expression as neutral as possible.

"Okay, rest. We'll start again—"

"When I'm ready."

I walk away, leaving him standing behind, the distance between us more tangible than ever.

I can't deny this anymore. I've already come to terms with the fact that I like him. But I also can't pretend I'm not angry at myself. How did I let myself get here?

A part of me wants to turn and see him standing there, but I don't. Even so, I can feel his eyes on me as I continue moving past the trees and out of sight. When I know he's gone, I lean against the tree, taking a few deep breaths. For a moment, I think I'll cry. But I surprise myself when I don't. Instead, I give myself permission to feel everything. One of the greatest lessons my mom and sisters taught me is not to run from my emotions. Even though he doesn't feel the same, my feelings are still valid. I'm allowed to feel whatever I need to feel.

However, the knowledge doesn't take the pain away. It doesn't make this any easier. It doesn't soothe the burn or help me breathe easier. Maybe one day I will be able to look at him and not feel hollowed out inside. But today is not that day. So, I square my shoulders and march down the avenue of limes. At least the water will be happy to see me.

MAYBE I'VE PUT TOO MUCH PRESSURE ON MYSELF, OR MAYBE I'M not putting enough. But a week later, I finally seem to find a break. I've barely slept and it's starting to show, but my friends are letting me deal with this in my own way, and I'm thankful. Both Jade and Noel have been a little extra clingy, but I forgive them. It's not like it's a bad thing to be surrounded by people who have your back.

Ben has become one of those people as well. Even Owen, although very stoic and one to keep to the background, has been watching out for me. Aiden must've realized just how badly I needed my space. Or maybe Natalie is keeping him so busy he doesn't have time to think about me. Either way, I'm trying to deal, so library and research have become my friend. Because without those books I wouldn't be able to survive. It's too easy to get lost in my head. I excel at overthinking.

When I think it's another night of nothingness, I stumble onto a story. Since starting my research, I have learned the best place to find information about the Ancients is in human stories. It's as if the Ancients were so unconcerned with the mundane population, they didn't bother covering their tracks. Which helps me.

The cover is old-timey, brown leather with intricate vine designs spreading out across the front and back. When I open the front page, the title is written in old English, an artwork all on its own. The letters are elaborate and fill up most of the space, *Stories of Olde*. The table of contents is full of story titles, most I've never heard of. As I browse through them, one catches my attention.

Orcnéas fram se Niht.

The words seem familiar, so I grab one of the many dictionaries on the table and start leafing through it. When that one doesn't yield results, I move to the next one. It's the third one that is finally old enough to give me a good translation.

"Monsters of the Night," I mumble out loud, breaking the silence. My eyes fly up to glance around, as if my disturbing the peace may offend someone. But I've been coming here by myself for days. I have nothing to fear. Instead of dwelling on that fact or the feelings of loneliness it brings, I grab the old book once again and turn to the story.

My heart squeezes in awareness as I try to make out the words. Dad taught me some of them, but he can read old English fluently and the pang grows more painful as I think of him.

I wish he was here.

I wish I could talk to him.

I will never not miss him.

Pushing the thoughts and emotions away, I focus back on the

page in front of me. Grabbing one of my notebooks and the oldest dictionary, I get to work. It seems like hours before the words begin to take shape. My excitement reignites the more I translate and soon, I can't even sit still. This story is everything I've been looking for. A part of me wonders if others in this book may provide even more information. But for now, this may be enough.

Because what is does is spark an idea. Something I may have learned from my sisters.

There are plenty of spells in these books, more than enough information to create something greater still. With my family working on the ancestry aspect, I can work on perfecting my spell work.

I've never been great at it. Harper is much better at words than I am. But what if I was able to create a spell like a story? What if I was able to pull the Ancients into the pages of a book?

The story in front of me tells of the monsters that came in the night. They were feral creatures who roamed the forests and stole into the houses through the shadows. They preyed on human spirit and human flesh. Nothing could keep them out, not when they set their sights on their prey. Yet, some fought back. The humans found ways to protect themselves. They sang songs and they told stories and the creatures left, driven away by the imagination and the love in each spoken word.

Sitting back, I let that information sink in. Harper has always loved books, just like our father. It's something they shared and some of that has been passed on to me. But I've never been the one for beautiful prose. Or even regular spell casting. I use what is already written or what I have already been told.

But as I mull over these stories and the people who lived centuries ago, I feel inspiration knocking on the doors of my mind. It's like all of a sudden, I have to try, or I will go insane.

Grabbing my notebook once more, I jot down a few words that rush into my mind. I don't stop to second guess myself but allow the words to flow, if only to help me understand this magic. It's as if I'm telling myself this story now, for the very first time.

When I'm finished, I've only written a few sentences, but they speak to me on a higher level, and I wonder if there is magic on the page the way it used to be. There's no way I could story cast, but I did write something important. Of that I have no doubt. It's more than a feeling. It's a certainty deep within my veins. I know exactly what I need to do next.

❧ 28 ❧

The next morning I'm at the headmaster's office before the sun even rises. Even Miss Cindy isn't at her desk yet.

"Miss Hawthorne, to what do I owe this pleasure?" Headmaster Marković greets me as he walks up to his office doors.

"What do you know about story spell casting?"

The man in front of me has never shown even one glimpse of surprise in the almost two years I've known him. Until now. His eyebrow twitches just enough that I know I said something he wasn't expecting to hear. I've barely registered his surprise before he masks it.

"I am not sure..."

"Please, with all due respect," I interrupt, before he can deliver whatever practiced excuse he has up his sleeve. "Don't hide the truth. I think this can really help us. I even wrote out the opening lines."

That stops him cold. This time, he doesn't even try to hide his surprise.

"You wrote out the beginning of a story spell?"

"Yes. It just came to me."

There's a tense pause, and it's like everything around us has gone completely still. I'm afraid to breathe too loudly as I wait for

Headmaster Marković to speak. He studies me for another moment before he reaches for his door and unlocks it, motioning me inside.

The lights come on automatically, magic or modern amenities, I'm not sure. He heads for the drink cart on the other side of the office, pouring himself a cup of tea. Even from the distance, I can see the water is steaming hot, and once again I'm amazed at the magic of this place.

"May I ask how you found out about story spell casting?" Headmaster Marković asks after taking a tentative sip of his tea. He turns to me, watching me as he waits for an answer. Then, as if remembering my presence, he motions to the cart, and I shake my head.

"I'm okay, thank you."

He heads back to his desk as I try to find a way to explain to him my discovery. Already the magic of the library is preventing me from uttering any of yesterday's events. But headmaster doesn't push me, as if he knows I'm struggling.

"I have come across some information," I say, and the words taste true on my tongue. "When I decided to put the information to practice, there was no hesitation in my magic. It just happened."

He stays silent for a moment longer, taking a few sips of his tea, mulling over my words. I didn't exactly provide much to work with but maybe it's enough. Finally, he places the cup on a saucer and leans back in his chair.

"Story spell casting is an old practice, older than you can imag- ine," he begins, his eyes on something in the distance, as if he's remembering that very time as a firsthand participant. "Not everyone is gifted with the power of storytelling that is required of such spells. Many feared the intensity of the magic that came with those castings. Since it was so unique, it was just as feared as the Ancients. Back then, people spoke of the Ancient evil. Not as much as they could have, considering the protective spells were already in place. But more so than they do now. Story spell casting was one of the ancient arts, and those who did not understand it, feared it so."

"What happened?"

"Story casting was banned. Those who practiced it were dubbed evil worshipers, those who possessed dark magic. Chaos ensued and so, story casting became obsolete. At least, in the magic world."

"What do you mean?"

"The non-magical society has kept records of magic for as long as we have been on this earth. Some may have no knowledge of such things. But others have created their own societies to help us keep the records straight. To us, these are treasured texts."

I don't interrupt again, letting the headmaster find his own pace and his own words. I'm getting slightly impatient, when he speaks up again.

"Have you ever read the story of Beowulf?"

"Of course. We studied it in English class."

"What you studied was an ancient story spell, one that tells a tale of a mighty warrior, but also teaches the ways of casting."

"He was magical?"

"He was. Many of those whom you have read about were magical. Or had magical help. At one time, the world knew of supernaturals and lived in peace with them."

Headmaster's words stop whatever questions have sprung to mind. Living side by side with humans with nothing to hide? It's a concept I cannot wrap my mind around. Even though I come from a town that is very understanding and has broken through a lot of the prejudice within our magical community, it still doesn't seem possible.

"But how?"

"I wish I could give you a plausible explanation. But in all honesty, that kind of a unity is foreign even to me." He takes another swig of his tea, his eyes focused on something over my head. "For as long as I have been the headmaster here, and even when I myself was a student, magical and non-magical communities have warred. They have warred within themselves, and they have warred with each other. When the Ancients roamed the earth, it was not always so."

"Are you saying the Ancients have been awake since their original slumber?" I sit forward, leaning my hands on the desk. This is a completely new piece of information to me as I have been led to believe this is the first time they have risen up.

"They have. Not to this extent." Headmaster focuses on me once more. "I am telling you this, Miss Hawthorne, because I believe you have the drive to find the answers we so desperately seek. You have also clearly been granted access to areas of this school I myself am not privy too. But I ask you, please, keep this knowledge to yourself. It will only lead to mass panic."

He watches me steadily, waiting for me to agree, and I do so because I understand panic all too well. We still have no idea who they have on the inside, or how to protect this school from a full assault from the Ancients. There is no doubt in my mind it is coming. It's not like we can tell them to go away.

The idea sparks before I can fully form it, and I sit up straighter. Headmaster Marković notices my sudden intensity but doesn't ask, waiting on me to share.

"What if I wrote a story casting spell for the school?" I ask, not sure where exactly I'm going with this, but I know it's right the moment I speak the words. As I meet Headmaster's eye, I realize he's waiting for me to continue. "There has to be a way to protect this campus once and for all. What if a story casting spell is the spell you've been looking for? It could work, right?"

"It could," Headmaster replies slowly, mulling over his next words, "But it is incredibly risky. Story casting has not been practiced for generations. There are rules upon rules."

"But I think it's worth the risk. Don't you?" He meets my eye again and I'm ready for it. Something in me is refusing to back down. "If the lives of all these students are on the line, shouldn't you do whatever it takes to protect them? And I'm not saying you haven't," I hurry on to add when his eyes flash for a second. I don't want to make him mad, but I truly believe in what I'm saying. I have no idea where this is coming from, but I trust it. I trust myself. "This could be our shot."

"You make a valid point, Miss Hawthorne," Headmaster Marković finally says, and I feel like I'm out of breath just from waiting for him to speak. "I will bring it before the council, and we will go from there."

"That is all I ask." I smile, feeling better for it. A part of me feels like I've finally done something to help. I can't seem to save my dad, but maybe I can do something for the school. For my friends and those I care about. Standing to go, Headmaster Marković stops me when he calls my name.

"Story casting is no joke," he says, looking me straight in the eye as he stands behind his desk. "Your ancestors carry the magic within them, and so it seems, do you. That is the only reason I can see the truth has been revealed to you. But Miss Hawthorne, beware. It is not something that is to be taken lightly."

"Understood," I reply, reaching for the doorknob. "Thank you."

I don't wait for him to say anything else or offer any other warnings. It's not like I think I've suddenly developed some super-powers that will solve all our problems. But it also doesn't mean I'm just going to sit on this knowledge. Like he said, those books told me the truth for a reason. I can't let my ancestors down.

⚜

THE WHOLE DAY HAS GONE BY AS A BLUR. I'M ITCHING TO GET back to the library, but I promised Jade that we would have a picnic in the meadow before the weather turns completely to winter. My friends need this shred of normalcy, and I'm not about to deny them that.

"Do you think things will ever go back to normal?" Jade asks, leaning over Noel to grab a bag of chips. It's the usual crew out here, Vera and Christy are present too. But we're not the only ones who are desperate for normalcy because there are a few other groups out and about around us. While the weather is still dark and gloomy, it's a little lighter than it's been.

"I don't know, Jade," I reply honestly, watching two girls and two guys throw a football around. "This may be our new normal for a while."

It's not what they want to hear, but it is the truth. We can't pretend our lives haven't been flipped upside down and the place that was supposed to be our salvation has become a target.

"Can you please stop being depressing?" Christy whines from the other side of the blanket. She's just as dramatic and over the top as usual, and I chuckle. "Let's play a game! I know Noel brought cards."

"That I did." He pulls out a few decks without hesitation, and I smile. It's crazy how you may know someone for such a short time and yet claim them as your own. Unwillingly, my mind drifts to Aiden. A part of me has begun thinking of him as exactly that, and while it wasn't smart, it's not something I could've controlled. Or maybe I should've. It would help to have my sisters here to navigate the madness of boys, but at least I have my girls. And Noel. I do feel like I can talk to him about this as well. Even though I think our next conversation should be about him finally making his move on Jade. He'll be pining forever if he doesn't step up.

I'm still thinking about my two best friends when I feel a prickle at the back of my neck. The rest of the group begins to argue about what game they want to play, but I'm no longer listening. Something is coming, or maybe it's already here. I can feel it like a rumbling under my feet. As I study those around me, I realize the shifters are out and about as well. I didn't notice them earlier, besides the regular patrols, but now I see they're everywhere. My eyes land on Owen first before I find Ben. There's no happy go lucky expression on his face. He's all business, and that makes me that much more worried.

A sudden shriek pierces the near silence, and I twist around to try and find the source of it. Rain drops from the sky as if being spilled from buckets, soaking us in mere seconds.

"What's happening?" Vera shouts, and even this close to her, it's difficult to make out the words as a full-blown storm descends on us in seconds. Jumping to my feet, I squint through the sheet of water, calling on my magic at the same time. But nothing happens. It's like my magic is being blocked.

"I can't stop it!"

"What?"

People are running in every direction, but the main building is too far, and the storm is becoming stronger by the second.

"We have to go!" I scream, trying to be heard over the pouring rain. The storm continues to rage, making it difficult to see five feet ahead. I wave my arms, trying to get everyone's attention. There's only one place we can go.

"Come on!"

With Jade close on my heels, I race toward the building I spent most of my afternoons in. Others seem to pick up on our intention, and they turn toward the building as well.

Chaos bombards us on every side, but I don't slow down. When Jade slips beside me, I grab her before she can faceplant, pulling her after me. Ben and Owen are suddenly by our side and then Aiden is there as well. The wind howls, nearly sweeping me off my feet and trying to push me in the opposite direction. I grip Jade's hand and beg for my magic to do something, but it merely reaches a foot in front of me before I feel resistance.

The house outline can be seen through the rain but barely. Others are rushing in, stumbling over each other as they try to get out of the storm. We burst through the doors as one, pushing past all the people. Aiden, Ben, and Owen are the last ones inside, barricading the door behind them.

"Stand back!" I command, and the boys move as one. I focus on my magic, trying to find my center. Whatever is blocking me outside is not about to win in here. Now that I have a second to concentrate, I let my magic reach out, pushing past the resistance.

Already, I can tell my magic alone won't be enough, but there is one other thing I can try. Taking a deep breath, I call on my ancestors to help and guide me, hoping I'm doing the right thing. It's not like my sisters got back to me with a manual. Even so, I feel my magic grow a tad stronger, and I hold onto that.

"Protect, protect, protect," I whisper right as I thrust my hands forward, sending the magic flying. It smacks into the doors and spreads out around us, sealing us inside. The spell drains me instantly, and I stagger on my feet. Aiden moves towards me but stops himself as Ben reaches me first.

"I'm okay." I smile at the shifter, but I think it comes out more like a grimace because he doesn't seem reassured. A growl reaches my ears, and I glance up just in time to watch Aiden march toward me with a determined look on his face. He pushes past everyone, sweeping me off my feet and into his arms. I gasp, wrapping my arms around his neck automatically.

It takes my brain a second to catch up to what's happening, as everyone stands a little shocked around us.

"Umm, put me down," I finally say, finding my words.

"You're dead on your feet, Duchess," he replies, stepping around my friends as he carries me to one of the couches in the next room.

"Aiden."

"Maddie."

He doesn't let go until he's standing over the furniture. But even then, he hesitates. I try not to think about the way he cradles me against his chest or the gentle way he's supporting my body. When I meet his eye, a touch of concern can be found there. It moves straight into my heart and grows as he gently sets me down. His face hovers over mine, his gaze intense. If I move even a fraction of an inch, our noses will brush. It takes all my self-control not to pull him toward me. I think he can see the desire in my eyes and his own flash in response.

Just then, the building shakes from an impact, jarring both of us out of our staring contest. My gaze falls over his shoulder, landing on my friends who have followed us into the room. Jade's eyes are sparkling, and Noel looks a little worried. And also fearful. Actually, they all look scared.

"What is that?" Vera asks, pushing farther into the room and past my open-mouthed best friends.

"The shadow creatures," I reply automatically, orienting myself on the couch. Aiden has moved away as if he's been burned by touching me and is now standing by the opposite wall. "They're trying to get past the spell."

"How do you know?"

"I've seen them in person before. I wasn't sure until just now, when I focused on my magic. They're known to syphon magic, and it's the same kind of resistance I found when I looked."

"This building has the same protection as the main school though, right?" Jade asks, taking a seat beside me.

"It does. But I added something extra."

We're all exhausted. There are students huddled all over, wet and shivering from the cold. This attack took us completely by surprise. And that should be impossible, considering we've been walking on eggshells all semester.

"So, does that mean they can't get in at all?" Christy asks from her position by the door. She looks so small, half covered in dirt, with her arms wrapped around her middle. I want to reach out and comfort her, but all I can offer her are my words.

"Someone would have to physically open the door from in here to penetrate my spell. So even if they bust through the school's magic, we have an extra layer of protection." She nods, and I can see her shoulders drop a little. Vera and Noel both look just as reassured as Christy. The shifters, on the other hand, are still on full alert.

"What happened out there?" I ask, directing my question at Ben. But the moment he opens his mouth, Aiden steps in.

"They've been on the outskirts of the magical shield for days," he says, crossing his arms in front of him as he leans against the door. "Headmaster called us in a few hours ago to double the patrols. They were planning some kind of spell when the creatures broke through. They started attacking people directly, and you're right, taking their magic. It happened so fast, it's as if they knew exactly where to find them, and the sudden storm provided the cover."

I close my eyes briefly as he speaks, picturing the scene. I was only privy to our part in it, and it happened so quickly, no one had any time to react. If this is the same around the whole campus, the shadow creatures would have a feast.

The spell Aiden is talking about must be the story casting one the headmaster was supposed to present to the council. Everything is happening at once, no wonder we're struggling to stay ahead of the game. We don't even have time to do proper research.

Just then, another impact shakes the walls around us, and Jade grabs my hand. She's not even hiding the fact that she's terrified. My body feels the drain on my magic, and I feel weaker than I should be. I glance at Aiden who's been watching me this whole time, and I want to ask why he was in the meadow when he could've been stationed anywhere else. But then I notice Christy sliding carefully toward the doors to the hallway.

"Christy?" I call out, and the girl turns right as she steps through the doorway. "Everything okay?"

She gives me the sweetest of smiles before replying, "It will be."

Something doesn't feel right. I untangle my arm from Jade and push to my feet. Somehow Aiden is right beside me in an instant as I wobble, but he doesn't reach for me. However, his presence soothes my nerves, but I'm not about to tell him that. Instead, I push past him and into the hallway.

"Christy," I call out, pausing on the other side of the doorway as the petite girl makes her way slowly down the hallway. "What are you doing?"

She stops right in front of the door to the outside, placing her palm against the wood as if she's feeling the building tremble through her fingertips. Cocking her head so she can look at me over her shoulder, she smiles big and my blood runs cold.

"Letting them in, of course."

Before anyone of us can move, she grabs the handle, pulling it open. My spell dissipates, and with it, our protection.

The traitor has been under our noses this whole time, and she just broke the last layer of our defenses.

❦ 29 ❦

A iden and Ben growl on either side of me before launching themselves forward. Christy raises her hands, and both shifters hit an invisible wall at once, sliding back toward me. I drop to my knees, my hands on each of them as they shake off the impact.

"Funny Maddie," Christy says, and her voice doesn't sound like her own. "Always trying to save people and... creatures." My hand is still on Aiden's upper arm, and I drag him to a standing position beside me. Owen helps Ben up, and both of them take their position at my back, with Aiden at my side.

"It was you the whole time," I say now, and the other girl laughs like she's a villain on a bad TV show.

"Of course it was me. And you had absolutely no idea. You were too busy with your stupid schoolwork and your unrequited love crushes and sucking up the headmaster, you golden child."

It's hard not to look at Aiden at Christy's words, but I can feel his eyes shift to me. I'm sure he's putting two and two together. She's not exactly being subtle.

"Why?" I have to keep her talking while we figure out what to do next. But it's not like I can communicate telepathically with the shifters. My plan will have to be my own. Everyone else has moved away from the main hall as the wind blows all around Christy. If I look closely enough, I can make out the shapes of the shadow creatures at her back, but it's like she's keeping them in check for the moment.

"Why not?" She laughs again, and I'm really starting to hate that sound. "You thought you were the big man on campus after that little spell you and your sisters pulled but look at you now. You couldn't' even see what was staring you right in the face."

I shake my head, amazed at how focused she is on this concept of my popularity. "You really think I wanted all this responsibility?"

"Ha! You've been eating it up all semester. Woe is me, I'm Maddie Hawthorne, a powerful witch with a super cool spell under my belt. Don't look at me. Well, only when I want you to."

Bitterness drips off her every word, and I don't know what to say to that. How can I explain to her my actual feelings on the matter when she has already made up her mind about me?

"Is that what this is all about?" I wave my hand in the direction of the open doors, and the smile she gives me chills me to the bone.

"Of course it's not all about you, Madison," she says my name like a curse.

"So, what was it? Why betray this place? Why now?" I can't risk looking at the shifters, but I can feel them move at my back. Aiden's fingers graze mine, sending a million electric shocks up my spine, and the moment makes me braver. I take a step toward Christy, putting my friends at my back.

"You had to go and open your big mouth." Christy spits in my direction, all trace of that cute, bubbly girl gone from her eyes. "The council has been deliberating, and I can't let them spell extra protection over Thunderbird Academy."

So, Headmaster Marković stayed true to his word and went to the Elders. But how could Christy know any of this? And why is she involved?

"What's in it for you?" I ask, even though I have a pretty good idea.

"Power, of course. Ultimate power. They sure know how to reward their followers. And I? I will have no problem knocking down whatever spell you throw my way. Because I will be more powerful than you."

It's that simple. Power really does corrupt.

I move closer still, and this time, she notices.

"I wouldn't if I were you." She raises her right arm into the air, and I watch as three shadow creatures appear from the darkness at her back. "You know my dear friends, right?" Christy asks, that sinister smile back on her face. "They've been dying to say hello."

Before I can figure out what she means, she flicks her hand, and the creatures attack. Along with the first three, a dozen more pour into the building with Christy standing by the doors, laughing like a maniac. I can't tell if she's controlling them completely or only providing a pathway, but I know I have to get to her.

The chaos around me is a battlefield. The shifters have all turned and are holding their own against the Ancient's minions. I can feel the vibrations of battle magic echoing around me as my friends and fellow students fight the dark creatures. The storm is now inside the building as well as outside the walls. The blackness of the night is seeping into every nook and cranny, as if the mere presence of the Ancient magic is poisoning the land.

"Aiden, watch out!" My heart jumps inside my chest as I thrust my hands out in front of me, throwing up a protective shield right before the creature attacks Aiden from behind. The wolf spits out the creature he has in his mouth, dissipating the magic before he turns to look at me. Even in his wolf form, I see the gratitude and determination in his eyes. Suddenly they narrow, just as I feel something coming at me from the left.

I twist around, throwing up a protective shield, but I'm a second too late. I go flying across the hall, my back slamming into a wall. Dazed, I do my best to get up on all fours, but with my magic drained and my head spinning, I'm not fast enough. The tendrils of a shadow creature wrap around my wrists yanking me back. I cry out, searching for my battle magic, but I can feel it leaving me by the second.

The pain is excruciating, as if one of my limbs is being pulled clean off. Writhing on the floor, I try to clear my mind enough to think, but no dice. It's too much, all at once, and it feels like I'm being torn apart.

Then, just as suddenly, the pain is gone, and I open my eyes to find Aiden ripping the shadow creature apart. Since they're made of magic, all they do is reform somewhere else, but at least I'm no longer attached to one. That's when I realize what I need to do.

"Aiden," I say, getting to my knees. The wolf stops in front of me, and this time I don't hesitate. I plunge my hand into his fur, memorizing the silky texture with this one touch. Electricity sparks between us, but before I can understand it, I breathe easier as I meet his eye.

"Shadows cannot live in the light," I say, staring right at him. He nods, understanding exactly what needs to be done. "Give me five minutes."

⚜

AIDEN DOESN'T HESITATE TO STEP IN FRONT OF ME AS I GET TO my feet. One howl and Ben and Owen are suddenly there as well, protecting me from every side. I glance around, trying to find my friends, and see Jade and Noel battling a few of the creatures farther down the hall. Some students are screaming as the monsters eat their magic right up. The sight breaks my heart, but the only thing I can do for them now is draw out the shadow creatures. For that to happen, I need more power.

"Get me to Jade," I say, and the wolves move as one as I race behind them. Throwing up a protective shield, I wish for more water, but I make do with what I have. The rain outside is enchanted, so it's no use to me. When we're almost to my friend, something knocks me off my feet. I drop fast and hard while my face stings from the impact. With my head ringing, my instincts take over, and I pull on all those hours of working with Aiden.

I'm being straddled, and my neck is wrapped in a tight grip, so I do the only thing I can. I drive my palm straight up with full force and am satisfied when I hear a crunch and then a scream. Christy is immobilized for only a second, but it gives me enough time to find my momentum and push her off me. I'm on my feet as she recovers, blood dripping down her pink shirt.

"You broke my nose, witch," she spits, looking less like a human by the second. She's more of a feral creature than any animal I've ever seen, and that makes her dangerous.

"It looks better that way," I reply, unable to help myself. She doesn't like that, so she launches herself at me with a scream, but this time I'm prepared. Ducking underneath, I twist around, bringing my leg up to slam it into her back. She staggers forward but doesn't drop, and before I can deliver another kick, she's coming at me once more. I block her advances as she continues to swing her arms. For someone so small, she's incredibly strong and quick. I wouldn't be surprised if she's had a few magical enhancements.

When my fist connects with her face, I don't hesitate to grab her hair and pull her down as I bring up my knee. The impact affects both of us, but I manage to stay on my feet. She reaches for my skin, ripping half my shirt off and scratching up my arm, but I'm so focused, I don't even feel the pain. I punch her again before I knee her in the stomach, and I finish it with a jump kick. She lands hard on her back, completely knocked out, and I gulp air like a drowning man.

"Jade!" I call out when I find my voice again, and I turn in time to see Aiden and Ben take care of another three shadow creatures. With two leaps, Aiden is beside me once more, and I swear he looks proud of me when his gaze moves from my face to that of Christy's body.

"I told you I was paying attention," I mumble and then take off toward my friends.

"Jade, Noel, I need you," I shout, stopping near the doorway to the other room. They hear me and instantly move toward me as I turn to study who else is there. Vera has shifted into a hawk, and is a beautiful bird, much larger than any I've seen before. She's holding her own, but I need her witchy powers right now.

"Witches, I need you!" I shout into the room and a few students glance up at me before moving forward. Some are still fighting, but others race to meet me at the doorway.

My thought is simple. If I can call on my ancestors for help, then I can call on my fellow students as well. We need a blinding enough light to drive out the creatures, and I've only heard of the magic my sister's friend created month ago. Now, I get to improvise.

"Join hands," I direct as the shifters do their best to keep the creatures away from us. "I will call on the guiding light, and I need you to let me connect to your magic as an amplifier."

"How do we do that?" Noel asks as he takes Jade's hand. Vera lands elegantly beside him and shifts before she replies.

"Give Maddie permission to enter." She nods at me as she steps over and takes my hand. She's more powerful than I imagined considering she holds her clothes within her shift. That's usually the sort of magic that is earned, and if we survive this, I have a lot of questions for her. Now, I give her a soft smile, and then turn to face the main hallway. Jade grips my hand tightly, and I watch the rest of the witches follow suit.

Now that Christy is out of commission, it's as if the shadow creatures are given to their own devices. Those who are still fighting glance over at us and push the creatures out further, giving us a wider berth. The shifters are right in front of me, holding their own. When I take a deep breath, Aiden turns suddenly, his attention entirely on me.

I meet his eye, as if we're the only two people in the whole world, and this war is not happening around us. I find calm within the storm just by looking at him, and instead of hiding from the feeling or running from it, I embrace it.

It blossoms inside of me like a flower opening its petals, and my magic follows suit. My arms vibrate from the power of it all as I feel the students at my back giving me permission to enter. When I open my mouth, I'm still looking at Aiden.

"The night is dark, the evil is Ancient,
"But bonds are stronger than those of the agents.
"The story of old has all but been told,
"And the magic of sunrise has never been wronged."

The words of the story pour out of me as the ground under our feet begins to shake. The shadow creatures all pause, as if they feel something coming. I'm not about to disappoint them. The simplest of spells are sometimes the most powerful. I grin, my body beginning to glow from within, and then I utter the words.

"Let there be light."

❧ 30 ❧

When the blinding light finally dissipates, I drop down to my knees, completely spent. My friends are there to hold me up and then, so are the shifters.

"Maddie, you did it. They're gone," Jade whispers, hugging me tightly. I can barely hold my head up, but when I do look outside, I find the storm has ended, and it once again looks like a gloomy afternoon outside. I feel a slight bump on my arm, and I look over to find Aiden pressed against me. This time, I'm sure his wolf looks proud of me, and I manage a smile.

"Not bad, huh?" I ask, right before I pass out.

When I wake up, I'm in my room with no recollection of getting there. My body feels heavy, as if something is pressing on me at every side, but I don't actually feel any physical pain.

"You're awake!" Jade exclaims, jumping off her bed and coming to stand beside mine. "Oh Maddie, you really saved us. You're amazing!" She falls right into me, hugging me tightly, and I return the gesture.

"What happened?" I ask when she finally pulls back.

"I can't believe it was Christy all along," Jade comments, tears running down her face. "We trusted her, Maddie. How could we not see?"

"She didn't want us to see," I reply, sitting up fully and reaching for Jade's hand. "What happened to her?"

"Headmaster Marković and the council took her to prison. You really did a number on her. I think she'll be in recovery for a very long time. Part of her punishment is being stripped of her powers, and they're not performing any healing spells on her either."

"What about everyone else?"

"We've all been checked over by the healers. They're more concerned with our safety than anything else. Since the protective wards were breached, it's hard to rebuild them now. Especially since so much of the magic was drained during the battle. Headmaster, along with most of the staff and shifters, has been on patrol nonstop."

"Wait, how long was I out?"

"Almost a full day." Jade squeezes my hand. A day? I can't believe it. I need to get to the headmaster. I need to see what the council said about story spell casting. I need to see Aiden. That last thought comes unbidden, but I can't deny it. Something happened between us in that building, and I can't exactly run from it now. It felt more powerful than magic.

"Aiden has come by to check on you every chance he gets," Jade comments, as if reading my mind. She gives me a small smile, and I return it.

"I need to see him."

Without hesitation, Jade moves out of the way, so I can stand. Pulling on my jeans and a hoodie, I find that even though my body feels heavy, a part of me is energized. Something is happening to me, and I don't know if it's my own magic, or the story spell cast I used, but I feel... right somehow.

"He's scheduled to patrol by the pond," Jade says, as I lace up my boots. "He told me the last time he came in to check."

I give my friend a quick hug before I'm racing out of the room. The hallways are deserted, and I wonder if the students are barricading themselves inside their rooms, or holed up somewhere together. Clearly, we can leave our rooms, but I can understand why they wouldn't want to.

The few who are out and about patrolling don't try to stop me, but I can feel their eyes on my back. I have no idea if the rest of the school knows what I pulled in that building, but at this point, I'm used to the looks. After everything I've dealt with, I think I can handle a few stares.

I half walk, half sprint to the pond, passing a few of Aiden's pack mates in the process. They all seem to know exactly where I'm going. When I reach the pond, I find Aiden directly by the water.

"You're up," he says before turning to face me. I knew it wasn't just me who was so attuned to him that I could feel his presence. He doesn't move toward me, and now that I'm here, I freeze only five feet away. We study each other as if we've never seen the other person before. It's as if our eyes have been opened to something entirely new, and we're unsure of how to proceed from here.

"Thank you." I break the silence. "For what you did back there."

"I didn't seem to need to do much," he replies, flashing me a smile. I think my heart stops for a second at the sight, my eyes drinking in every detail. It's the first true smile I have seen from him and it shatters me into a thousand emotions. Suddenly, I can't seem to think, and I wonder if I look as flushed as I feel.

"You were incredible, Maddie," he continues, taking a tiny step forward. "I've never seen someone so in tune with their magic and so bold in their execution."

With each word, I think my world is tilting on its axis once more. If we don't get back to even ground, I don't think I'll ever be able to recover. So, I say the first thing that comes to mind.

"But the most important thing is how was my fighting form?"

There's a slight pause, and I think I'm just being stupid, but then Aiden laughs and the sound becomes my favorite sound in the world in a span of a second.

"Your fighting form was amazing. But it could probably still use some work."

It's my turn to laugh, and suddenly, I don't feel so awkward anymore. We were partners on that battlefield, and that means we will never be enemies again. This time, it's me who takes a step forward, and then we're only three feet apart. I don't want to push my luck, but I have to ask him. I have to know if I'm the only one thinking these crazy thoughts.

"That moment when I touched you, it—"

"I felt it everywhere," he interrupts, speaking softly, and now I know I didn't imagine the electricity rushing through me. He takes another step toward me, and now, the only thing between us is the air we share.

"What does it mean?" I whisper, afraid of the answer and afraid of not getting one.

"It can't mean anything," he replies, cracking my already fragile heart. But somehow, I don't move away, and Aiden is not done. "When I first saw you, it changed everything for me. I can't explain it, but it did. But you and I, we can only ever be this." He waves a hand between us, and somehow I understand. Seeing him has changed me too.

"I am bound by my duties as the next alpha, but I am also bound to the promise I made to make sure you are safe. Know that I will always keep that promise."

I frown at him, unsure of what he means by that last part. I know Natalie is part of his duty as the next alpha, and I know there's nothing I can do about that. I want to ask him about his promise, but just then a wolf runs over, and Aiden is back to his closed off soldier self.

"We need to go. Headmaster is looking for you," he says after he looks over at the wolf. I nod my head and swallow the tears that are threatening to overwhelm me. But before I can take two steps, Aiden does something that breaks me completely. He closes the distance between us and pulls me into his arms, much like he did after the dance. This time, he clings to me as tightly as I cling to him, and in this one embrace, I realize I've fallen in love with the alpha.

⚜

"WE CAN'T STAY HERE!"

The shouting greets us as Aiden and I reach the headmaster's office. Voices both male and female are talking over each other, and we push into the partially open door without an invitation. The moment we're inside, the arguing stops and the people in the room turn to face us as one.

Some of the teachers are here, but there are a few people I've never seen before. These must be the council members Headmaster was talking about.

"Miss Hawthorne, it is good to see you up and about." Headmaster Marković greets me warmly. I give him a small smile, still very unsure of myself in front of this group. He motions me closer, and when I walk farther into the room, I see that a few upperclassmen are here as well. Including Natalie. The other girl doesn't seem very impressed with me, but then again, I'm not impressed with her either.

"What possessed you to try story spell casting, girl?" One of the older women I've never seen before speaks, her voice full of disapproval. She appears to be in her seventies, her hair pulled so tightly into a bun, it makes my own scalp hurt. Her eyes are dark as she stares at me, waiting for an answer.

"Matilda, please," Headmaster Marković says, waving the woman off. "Miss Hawthorne saved her fellow students at the risk of her own health. That should be admired."

"It should be reprimanded. You have no idea what kind of power you are playing with here." There is so much venom in her words that it takes all the air from my lungs. But then, it makes me angry. This semester has taught me a lot about myself and one of those things is that I am braver than I give myself credit for. I'm not about to cower at the words of some old lady.

"Not to mean any disrespect," I begin, shocking everyone into silence. "But I didn't see you out there in the front lines, fighting to protect the students of this *fine* institution. I hope all the screaming and bloodshed didn't inconvenience you too much."

"How dare you?"

"No, I will not be spoken to like I'm some kid," I say, standing up a little taller. There's a light touch of a hand on my arm, and I realize Aiden is encouraging me with that small move. "I did what I had to do, and I would do it all again."

"Miss Hawthorne," Headmaster Marković interjects, shifting my attention to him. I'm pretty sure there's a gleam of approval in his eye, but I know he's not about to voice it. "What Elder Matilda is trying to say is, there are always consequences to this type of magic. Consequences that may not reveal themselves right away."

"I understand that, sir. And I will answer for those consequences when the time comes. But I will not apologize for saving my friends' lives."

"I told you, Henry. I told you!" Elder Matilda points her finger at the headmaster before she turns back to me. "She is unlearned and cannot be given the responsibility."

"That is your opinion, Matilda," Headmaster Marković replies. "And you are only but one vote."

"Headmaster, could you tell us what's happening?" Aiden says, voicing my own question.

"The council has voted to have Miss Hawthorne perform a story spell casting on the school." My heart leaps in my chest, elevated all at once. They're giving me permission to help. I was planning on doing so myself anyway, but this means I have their support.

"When can I begin?" I try not to sound too eager, but I can't hide my excitement.

"Immediately. We're on borrowed time here, and the wards could break down again at any moment."

"Wait a second." Aiden turns to me. "What exactly is story spell casting?"

"It's vile, and it has no place in this school," Elder Matilda spits, shooting daggers at me. I glance at the others in the room and find that the opinion seems to be divided. Most of my teachers look on with encouragement, as does one of the other Elders in the room. But the rest are very apprehensive, although not as hostile as Elder Matilda.

"It's an ancient way of spell casting that hasn't been performed in generations. But it's powerful, and it's what Miss Hawthorne did at the training building."

"But it nearly killed you!" Aiden's attention is entirely on me now, and he's not even trying to hide the worry.

"I'll be fine. I need to be more selective with my words. I think it only drained me so much because I was the conduit. If I use something else as an anchor, it won't be as bad." I try to reassure him, and I hope I'm making sense, because at this point, I'm making this up as I go.

"You need to be very specific with your words, Miss Hawthorne," Headmaster Marković agrees. "Next time, the aftermath of the spell could be much worse."

I understand what he means. I can die. I read about it in the books, not that I'm about to mention it now. But I don't think I need to. Aiden is a smart shifter. He knows what we're talking about. He opens his mouth to protest again, when the phone on the desk rings. Headmaster answers immediately, and only a few words are spoken before he turns to us.

"You need to start the spell immediately. More are coming."

❧ 31 ❧

They don't let me say two words before Mrs. Hously is guiding me into Headmaster Marković's chair. She hands me a piece of paper and a pen before she squeezes my shoulder.

"To tell a story you need a setting. Use the school as the basis, paint a picture. It doesn't have to rhyme, although poetry has always had the strongest affect in spell casting." She rattles off instructions hurriedly, her eyes shining with unshed tears. "Think of what matters the most. The greatest stories are filled with love and adventure. They're filled with heart. Find that and you will be fine."

My eyes drift to Aiden involuntarily, and I find him staring at me just as intensely. The teachers and staff hurry out of the room as Headmaster begins issuing orders.

"We need to keep the school as safe as possible until Miss Hawthorne is finished. Rally everyone. Every student, every magical being, tell them we are officially at war. I know they are scared, but if they have even a glimmer of magic, they are not helpless."

Miss Cindy rushes over to her desk and then the alarm begins to blare. Those in the room scatter quickly, each heading for their assigned areas.

"Mr. Lawson," Headmaster calls out, and I realize he's the only one, besides the Elders, left in the room.

"I'm staying with her."

He doesn't take his eyes off me as he says the words, and the intensity there takes my breath away. Then, Natalie moves from behind him, placing her hand on his arm.

"Your pack needs you, Alpha," she says, sparing me half a glance that's filled with so much hostility, I think my skin got burned.

"Miss Hart is right." Headmaster steps up, glancing between the two of us. "Miss Hawthorne is in capable hands."

I know he doesn't want to, but Aiden can't ignore the call of the alpha. He gives me one last heated look that's filled with all kinds of promises, before he's out the door.

"Now, Miss Hawthorne—"

"I'm on it."

Ignoring the angry glares from Elder Matilda, I concentrate on the paper in front of me. I am not a writer. Books are magic all on their own, and it's because of hard work and talent that authors create such stories. I think back to what Mrs. Hously said, that the best stories are filled with heart. And I know my heart belongs to this school.

It may not be anything I expected, and I never would've imagined this is where my life would lead me, but I love Thunderbird Academy. This place has been a home away from home, and I will not rest until it is a sanctuary once more.

I begin to write, letting those emotions guide my pen. When the screaming starts, I don't let up. Headmaster and the rest of the Elders, join hands, mumbling their own spell as I work on mine. I feel the magic fill this space, I hear the battle rage all around me, and yet I still write.

"Work faster, girl," Elder Matilda snaps, but even that sounds far away. I completely give myself over to the story. As the building begins to shake around me, I feel my heart bleed out into the words in front of me. When the last dot is on the page, I am spent. I glance up to find the Elders still in the midst of their spell, sweat running down their brows.

"Sir," I call out, afraid of breaking their concentration, but they don't answer me. "Headmaster Marković."

"Now, Maddie. Now," he calls, and I have no choice. Glancing down at the paper, I begin to read.

"There once lived a girl,
With magic in her veins,
Inside a castle made of stone,
On the grounds of Ancient remains.
The place has always been,
And the place will always be,
An institution of knowledge, of honor, of friendship,
Of tranquility.
Until the evil came and fought to destroy,
So, the girl took a stand and wrote a song.
It spoke of her happiness, of the friends she had made,
And it spoke of a boy, who had changed her fate.
She gave of herself, of her magic, her heart,
She did not hesitate to protect, to impart,
This story will not end with failure or pain,
The institution will withstand,
Just like witches, and shifters, and pixies, and fae.
There is nothing more precious than the love of a girl,
And there is nothing stronger than the bonds of a spell.
Protect, protect, protect."

As I read the words, the world around me shifts. I hear someone screaming my name, but I'm too lost in the story to care.

It's as if I am singing to a melody only I can hear, and when I'm done, everything feels right again. The paper falls from my hands, and I drop back down to the seat, my heart beating wildly, my body buzzing from the magic.

"Stupid girl, what did you do?" Elder Matilda is screaming as I focus back on the room. The others look horrified, and I don't understand what's happening.

"Headmaster Marković?"

He doesn't meet my eye but continues to stare out the window. I follow his gaze and find a forest I've never seen before on the other side of the glass. I no longer see the campus I have come to love, nor do I hear the sounds of struggle. Confusion clouds my mind as I glance down at the words I've written.

"What did I do?"

No one moves as a knock sounds at the headmaster's door. He walks over to it, pulling it open, and a person steps in. My mouth falls open at the sight, and at first, I think I'm hallucinating.

"Okay, which one of you have decided it would be a good idea to drop Thunderbird Academy in the middle of Spring Court's forest?"

I don't think I hear him right, and then it all falls into place. They warned me to be careful with my words and intentions. I wrote with my friends in my heart.

"Umm, Liam?" I stand, and the fae's eyes dart to me immediately. "I think that was me."

His eyes light up at the sight of me as his mouth breaks into a breathtaking smile.

"Maddie Hawthorne, why am I not surprised? I knew you wouldn't survive the year without me."

MADDIE'S LIST OF OLD SLANG
WORDS/PHRASES

Claws sharp - A lot of knowledge about various things.

Chicks on a raft! And Eggs on a toast! - diner speak, sometimes used as a utterance of surprise.

Made in the shade - Everything is going well and there is not a care in the world.

Don't have a cow - Don't get upset or go ballistic.

Peachy keen - very good.

Tickety-boo - everything is correct or everything is okay (depending on the situation)

Gigglemug - a perpetually smiling person.

Minding you Ps and Qs - "be on your best behavior", "mind your manners".

Dilly Dally - wasting time through aimless wanderings.

Pung Wangle live or go along cheerfully in spite of misfortunes.

Source: bustle.com, mentalfloss.com, first hand experiences.

NOTE FROM THE AUTHOR

Thank you for reading my book! If you have enjoyed it, please consider leaving a review. Reviews are like gold to authors and are a huge help!

They help authors get more visibility, and help readers make a decision!

And if you'd like to know what comes next, sign up for my newsletter! More books are coming!

http://eepurl.com/ioJC5

Thank you!

NEXT IN THUNDERBIRD
ACADEMY SERIES

Of Destiny and Illusions - coming January 2020!

Be the first to know by joining my newsletter or text message updates!

http://eepurl.com/10JC5

- https://slkt.io/C6B
or text VLindBooks to 31996

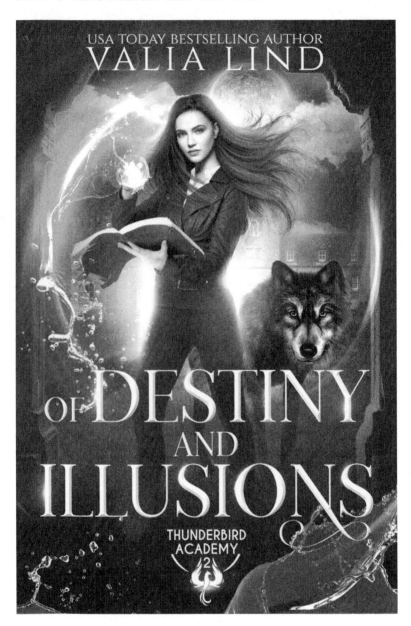

USA TODAY BESTSELLING AUTHOR
VALIA LIND

OF DESTINY
AND
ILLUSIONS

THUNDERBIRD
ACADEMY
2

ABOUT THE AUTHOR

USA Today bestselling author. Photographer. Artist. Born and raised in St. Petersburg, Russia, Valia Lind has always had a love for the written word. She wrote her first published book on the bathroom floor of her dormitory, while procrastinating to study for her college classes. Upon graduation, she has moved her writing to more respectable places, and has found her voice in Young Adult fiction. Her YA thriller, Pieces of Revenge is the recipient of the 2015 Moonbeam Children's Book Award.

Sign up to receive a text for new releases and sales!
- https://slkt.io/C6B
or text VLindBooks to 31996

ALSO BY VALIA LIND

Hawthorne Chronicles - Season One
Guardian Witch (Hawthorne Chronicles, #1)
Witch's Fire (Hawthorne Chronicles, #2)
Witch's Heart (Hawthorne Chronicles, #3)
Tempest Witch (Hawthorne Chronicles, #4)
The Complete Season One Box Set

Hawthorne Chronicles - Season Two
Of Water and Moonlight (Thunderbird Academy, #1)
Of Destiny and Illusions (Thunderbird Academy, #2) - coming January
2020!

The Skazka Chronicles
Remembering Majyk (The Skazka Chronicles, #1)
Majyk Reborn (The Skazka Chronicles, #2)
The Faithful Soldier (The Skazka Chronicles, #2.5)
Majyk Reclaimed (The Skazka Chronicles, #3)
Complete Box Set

Havenwood Falls (PNR standalone)
Predestined

The Titanium Trilogy
Pieces of Revenge (Titanium, #1)
Scarred by Vengeance (Titanium, #2)
Ruined in Retribution (Titanium, #3)
Complete Box Set

Falling Duology
Falling by Design
Edge of Falling

Printed in Great Britain
by Amazon